PROJECT BATTLE ROYALE

A Gamelit Survival Book

L.S. Halloway

Savage Tiki Time

To the Surf Bros

CONTENTS

1

Dropping In

The seats of the plane were packed tighter than a twelve pack of Mountain Dew. The air transport sat four to a row with an aisle that split them down the middle. Goemon and I ended up somewhere in the middle, but positioning did not matter so much. Passengers on this ride had the power to leave whenever they wanted.

The cabin lights did little more than stop people from bumping into each other. It might have been nice to use the downtime to check the gear on the other players, to see who was spending their allowance on skins and who was saving up to buy a crate and a key. The lurch of the plane and the overall darkness made it too difficult, though. I just focused on the map and the flightpath of the transport instead.

The cargo airliner appeared in the bottom left corner of the popped-up screen that was the map. It appeared to be headed at an almost exactly 45-degree angle across the map to the northwest. This meant nearly all of the First Island map was open for business- we could jump out and parachute far enough to make it anywhere. We called it First Island because it was the first island in the game and the real name was impossible to pronounce. In a few seconds, the plane would be over land.

The players onboard screamed and howled at each other in anticipation. The sound barely reached above the roar of the engines. Half the crowd failed to form words due to the sheer excitement, or possibly, stupidity. Some shouted general obscenities about each other's moms, or proclamations like "China number one!" More tried to bait players into dropping at a high population area like Big Town- "Meet me at Big Town or you don't have any balls," was the preferred method of communicating that sentiment. The rest, including Goemon and I, sat mostly silent, contemplating and planning the round by ourselves.

"Where do you wanna drop?" I asked.

"I don't know. The Spot?" Goemon said.

"We always hit The Spot. What if we mix it up?"

"Sure, why not? We can't do any worse than this streak."

"Alright. Here!" I said and placed a marker on the map for Goemon to see.

"Atlantis, huh? Risky, but I guess it's not Big City or Gun Range. I like it."

Amidst the yammering of players and the engines' wail, the cargo door of the plane opened up to let in some fresh air. Players began to leap out the back of the plane, most of them likely headed to Windy Harbor below. Sometimes dropping with the a huge group off the plane was good for a laugh. The problem was you usually end up with nothing but a crowbar to go along with some shotgun shells without the actual shotgun. Meanwhile, everyone else already has a fully-kitted M4 trained on your uncovered head and the round is over as soon as it began.

About a third of the plane had emptied out the back and the marker on the map approached fast. "Let's do this!" I yelled upon leaping out the back of the plane. Rather than take in the sights, I angled my body like a bullet straight down in order to maximize freefall speed. It worked in old secret agent spy movies and it worked here too. When I got oriented enough I looked back up for Goemon, who was not there.

"Where in the world are you going?" I screamed through the wind into the comlink.

"What? Oh, right," Goemon said calmly. I could see nothing but his displayed name in the distance. I opened the map and saw my partner had missed the drop point. Not by much, just a measly few thousand feet.

"Great, guess I'm going to get there first," I said while closing the map. Of course, that was wishful thinking. The parachutes of players who had dropped a few seconds sooner opened beneath me and filled the horizon. I would be the first of the duo to get there, sure, but I would be far from the first player to arrive at Atlantis.

To land in the middle of the city was suicide. First off, every building in the town had at least one window facing toward the center. This meant already equipped players just had to peek out of their respective houses for a free kill there first. Then there was the issue of a distinct lack of any serviceable weapons in the middle. To top it all off, the water ran deepest in the center, too. This caused a real issue with trying to actually move, and moving was a crucial part when it came to avoiding bullets.

My parachute deployed automatically once I fell close enough to ground level. With only a few seconds left before touching down, I tried to pinpoint where the closest threats would land. I counted six right off the bat, but had to stop when I realized where my landing trajectory was headed. The center of Atlantis, the big barrel of fish, sat right beneath. I banked left as fast as possible and smashed through the window of a building. It was not the most graceful landing, but it was better than ending up in that swamp.

Even though everyone else in the city knew where I was thanks to the crack of the shattered window, I opened the map one more time and marked the building for Goemon's sake.

"Try and land on the roof here, hurry. There's like ten

people in this city. This was a terrible idea," I said.

"Alright, just stay alive," Goemon responded.

"Good advice."

In the distance, the low burst of gunshots declared the official start of the round. It was always amazing how some players managed to not just land so quickly, but find, equip, load, and fire their weapons, too. At least the shots were far off- probably closer to Windy Harbor or The Big City- instead of in my humble home.

Speaking of a humble home, the first floor of my chosen building just so happened to be about three feet underwater. If there was any loot to pick up, I could not see it through the waist-high muck and did not want to waste any more time play- ing scrap diver. The first floor was a loss, but that was fine. There were two more floors to check just up the stairs.

Another duo was kind enough to tell me that they knew exactly where I was by launching hot lead through the broken window. They might have missed my body, but the jolt was enough to kick my heart into overdrive already. I ducked be- neath the window and watched more bullets whiz overhead. Judging by the angle and the sound, they must be on the top floor across the way- better than being right outside the door.

"I picked a real bad house," I said, just before taking a deep breath and bolting up the stairs. I checked my torso for a leak, but everything appeared intact for the moment.

"I'm about to land. Which building are you in?" Goemon said.

"The map! Look at the map!"

"The top building or the bottom building?"

"The top!"

Goemon landed on the roof of what he presumed to be the top building. Unfortunately, it was not the one currently occupied by me.

"You picked the wrong one!" I yelled.

"Oh, you meant the bottom one," Goemon replied. "Holy smokes, there's a ton of people here." He was scampering around the rooftop.

"I told you. Just find a gun and get over here, this house sucks, I've got nothing."

"There's...there's someone up here with me."

"Get out of there!"

"No time. I'm gonna have to get my hands dirty."

The second floor of my spot proved more fruitful than the first, if only slightly. The gunshots from the opposing White Building Duo ceased for the moment, thanks to my proximity to the dirty floor. They must have had a bad angle. I slipped on a level one vest, which worked about as well as an umbrella full of holes in the rain. It was better than nothing, though. The can of soda might not have been exactly what I needed at the moment but I grabbed it anyways. The ten rounds of shotgun ammo I collected hinted tantalizingly at the presence gun itself, but it was unfortunately absent. Finally, I found a Revolver and 15 rounds of ammunition for it.

"Oh shoot! He's trying to punch me," Goemon said.

"What did you think was going to happen?"

"I don't know. Get back! I've got a pan. Don't make me use this!"

Goemon failed to find a ranged weapon, but he found the next best thing: a cast iron frying pan. As far as melee weapons go, the pan sat alone at the top. It worked about as well as you might think heavy metal cookware would in a fight. However, it did a fine job of covering your rear end from sniper fire in the late game.

I loaded the Revolver with the knowledge that it would

not do much good against anyone with anything bigger. Still, it did instill some amount of confidence which did not exist at all only half a minute prior. In fact, I felt so good that I decided to peek out the window to take a closer look at White Building Duo who had me marked. They were still trained on the building, but were looking at the wrong floor. They had apparently lost the scent for the moment. Normally, I would take the opportunity to line up a perfect headshot with the Revolver, followed by firing and missing the shot far wide left while at the same time alerting everyone in a three mile radius, including the target, of my location. This time, I held off thanks to a shotgun-wielding intruder making his way up the stairs of the very building occupied by the duo that had so aggressively tried to fire at me. Karma came hard and fast in PBR.

Neither member of White Building Duo knew what was coming to them. They were simply too preoccupied with searching out the window- for me, most likely- to focus on any threat beneath them. The shotgunner sprinted up the stairs, spurred on by the knowledge that two distracted and therefore helpless targets waited on the next floor.

I turned back from the window and moved to the top floor as the sound of shotgun blasts rang out. The gunfight next door would buy more than enough time to get geared up for battle...if there was any gear to speak of.

"People are going down out there. People got auto shotties already. Are you still alive?" I asked.

"Yeah. I hit him once with the pan and then he just straight up jumped off the roof. Where you at?"

"I'm still in the same building I marked. Third floor. There is jack in here. Do you have a gun?"

"I have a pistol and a vest."

"Wait, shh."

The slap-thump of footsteps. But from where? They

sounded close, almost inside of the house, but that was impossible. The only way in was splashing through the water on the first floor. I hit the deck and listened intently for the source of the noise. I succeeded in getting my eardrums blown out by the sound of a spraying and fully automatic AK-47 nearby.

The racket of the AK joined with another, smaller rifle. Neither of them were aimed in my direction. So I snuck a glance through the window again. Two fresh duos had taken to the rooftops and spotted each other. Now their meeting was so great they decided to exchange hollow points as gifts. It did not matter who won the engagement, the victor had Goemon and I outgunned either way.

"I think we should bail out," I whispered into the comlink, as if the enemy duos could hear me over the gunfire.

"I was just thinking the same thing."

"I can dip out the back window. Can you make it?"

"Way ahead of you."

I crawled under the window and headed back down to the second floor. One window faced mayhem and bloodshed. The other, an open field and a fresh start. I hopped through the glass, shattering it with all the silence of the airliner they rode in on. Goemon was already waiting in the field, a Glock or something in his right hand.

"You can't use the front door?" Goemon said.

"Not if you want me to survive. Nobody heard me, they're too busy shooting each other to pieces. Let's get the heck out of here."

"Alright, where to?"

"Think we can make it to The Spot?"

"Might as well try."

2

Shacked Up and Good to Go

Goemon and I put our backs to Atlantis and sprinted. Two pairs of gunshots continued to sound off from behind. It was not soothing exactly, but there was something reassuring about the gunfire being in the opposite direction rather than dead ahead. Unfortunately, the dead zone between Atlantis and The Spot now loomed.

"We probably should have just landed there in the first place," I said.

"I mean, probably. But we always drop there," Goemon said. It was surprising, I figured he would have been bummed and eager to hassle me for making the terrible decision.

"I guess sometimes we gotta mix it up."

"Exactly. We'll bounce back, baby."

The punishment for dropping at Atlantis could have been worse. For starters, we both could have died right off the bat, like the Jungle Island fiasco. It doesn't get much worse than that. Or one of us could have died, and that was just as bad. Losing not just your partner but your best friend that early in the match made for a terrible round. Now all we had to do was hope The Spot still sat vacant, and a fully loaded duo was not headed in our direction.

The dead zone left no discernible towns separating Atlantis and our destination. We did the only thing there was to do: run like gazelles across the savanna. At least the grass provided plenty of cover for our ankles in case any sniper watching had a real problem with bare feet. The rest was completely exposed, and still helmet-less to boot.

"You see any cars?" Goemon yelled, his own head on a swivel.

"I think I see a motorcycle. No, actually that's just a rock," I sighed.

"Shoot. We have to try and find something. Maybe let's check the shacks."

"Sounds good."

Goemon arrived at the shack first. At only the size of a janitor's closet, the little structures typically did not contain much in them. On an average round, if you already had anything close to a rifle it was not worth stopping. This was no average round and our duo had nothing that resembled a rifle so it seemed worth it to stop.

I played watchman while Goemon searched the dilapidated shack. It was only built for one and really more of an outhouse than anything else. There were worse jobs than standing guard. Besides, the team worked better the faster Goemon got a gun into his hands.

"Oh, Baby with a capital B," Goemon shouted.

"What'd you get? Hurry up already."

"What's a three letter word for happiness?"

"Uh. Fun?"

Goemon pushed the door of the shack open and it fell off the hinges, smacking into the ground. "Close. But the answer is Uzi." He raised the small, ferocious, and altogether Chihuahua-like weapon in to the air as he emerged back into the plain. With his free hand he tossed a grenade to me, which I began to juggle back and forth in a panic. "Relax, it's not cooked. I thought you might need it."

"Jeez, thanks for giving me a heart attack," I said.

"Should we go to another shack?"

"I mean, I'd like a gun, too."

Another ramshackle establishment stood slouched on a small hill nearby. This one boasted as many as three walls, which made looting that much quicker. Unfortunately it made protection that much worse if anyone happened to be watching. This time I led the charge as we headed toward the embankment. I was desperate for something, anything better than the Revolver I had equipped. And the grenade did not count. I never did figure out the physics of how to throw them the right way.

Goemon brought a lot to the table in our rounds together. Sure, he could shoot straighter than I could and he had a careful patience that usually kept us both alive more often than my attention span did. But when we cruised around together either in game or IRL we carried an unbreakable sense of camaraderie. Even in empty expanses like the dead zone plains we found ourselves in, we moved and acted as one unit. We were always on the same page, no matter what. Plus, I always knew he had my back- I did not have to turn around to know he was there, even if I could hear his footsteps clear as a map marker in front of me. Except...those were not his footsteps. He was gone.

"Where are you going?" I heard him say over the comlink. I turned and saw my teammate headed in the other direction, about 50 meters from where I thought he should have been.

"There's someone here!" I tried to keep my voice down. "Right in front of me. West. I mean North. I mean, 45 degrees." I never could read the compass to make effective callouts under duress. I hit the deck, hoping they did not hear me as clearly as I heard them. I could tell they were close, either just on the other side of the hill or already on top of it. I slithered like a snake behind a tiny boulder that provided cover to about half of my body. It cost the ability to see the exact location of the approaching duo. "They're coming up the hill, going to the shack. The shack that we were supposed to be going to. Together."

"Oh, you meant *that* shack."

"Just get over here already."

I popped my head up from cover, glancing over the rock. Somehow, they did not know where I was, but it was only a matter of seconds before they finished looting the shack and headed down the hill.

"They're in the shack. I don't think they saw me," I said. I got brave, sat up on knee and aimed the Revolver.

Goemon must have seen me. "Don't you do it," he said. "Gimme two seconds."

I counted to two and fired down the sights, nailing my target with my first shot and missing the next two. The rival duo did not come out guns blazing, opting instead to hunker down in their miserable excuse for a fort. Goemon crouched a short distance away, using the angle of the hill as his only defense.

"Well, they know we're here now," he said.

"Yeah, but I shot one of them. Shoot that one. Besides, they don't know you're there. I'll distract them."

I took a couple more potshots through the empty wall, not really expecting to hit anything. The Revolver was not much good unless I could score a headshot, but I figured I could at least keep them pinned down or at the very least nervous under a steady stream of fire. The biggest problem was my wonky angle. They had no clear shot at me, but that meant I had no clear shot at them, either. What we needed was a fresh plan.

"I'm going to back up a little bit, try and draw them out," I said while I reloaded a six pack. I was eating up bullets like

Halloween candy, even though I had pretty much nothing in reserve storage. A short sprint behind me was another rock about the same size. It would not make my pistol any more effective, but I figured my opponents would think the same thing and they might feel emboldened to come after me. I turned and ran a zigzag pattern, hoping that the fact I did not see any long barreled rifles on them might keep me alive.

The buckshot hitting my feet told me two crucial things. One of them had a shotgun, not a rifle. It also told me that he took the bait. He must have been either bloodthirsty or not very smart, because a shotgun at that range, especially one without a choke, would have as good a chance taking me down as I did passing Physics without cheating. I'll give the player this, he did manage to hit me with a few pellets. The damage resulted in nothing more than a sliver off of my health bar.

While the shotgunner bounded and fired after me, Goemon prepared to spring into action. I dipped behind the rock to the soundtrack of lead pellets raining on stone. "His buddy is coming down to help. Better make it quick," I called out.

Right on time, Goemon let the Uzi loose. By the time the shotgunner knew he had been flanked, he was already downed by the rapid fire of the micro SMG. A knocked player could no longer attack, but they could still move around, albeit about as a fast as a peglegged tortoise. Getting knocked down also earned you something of a death clock. If your partner fails to pick you back up before your health bar ticks down to zero, that's it- the round is over for you. The more times you go down, the faster that death clock moves. Getting shot in that state pretty much ends the timer altogether.

Meanwhile I trained the Revolver's sights on the other guy running down the hill. Again I landed the first shot. Unfortunately, the mule kick of the Revolver threw off my aim again and my next few shots went wide. Recoil control had yet to become one of my strong suits.

Fortunately, Goemon and his Uzi were there to pick up the slack. This time his target was not distracted, and he had an SMG of his own. They both unloaded their magazines on each other, each scoring their own fair share of hits. I resisted the urge to take free shots at the downed shotgunner, who was currently crawling a futile escape into the empty field behind us. Instead, I decided to be a bigger man, put kill counts and scoreboards aside and focus on the immediate threat. I did this because I'm selfless, a real team player.

I softened the attacker with one more round and let Goemon finish him off. Just in time, too, because Goemon himself would have been knocked by one more bullet. The deed finished, both enemy players fell limp to the ground. A wooden crate- aka the loot box- appeared over both corpses. The loot box served two main functions: tombstone and treasure chest. PBR represented the idea that one man's misfortune was another man's gain better than just about any simulation in history.

"Get just absolutely destroyed," Goemon said. He was fired up, and for good reason. Early kills were crucial for a successful round. It was simple probability. If I did not shoot by the time we got down to the top 25 still standing- meaning I survived by hiding in a corner the whole round- I knew I would not shoot the whole game. It was simple probability: the less I fired, the more likely I was to get shot in the face by some sniper a mile away that I would never even see. On the flip side, getting kills early had a lovely snowball effect, in no small part due to the boost that it had on confidence.

We both knew that we had to loot quickly. Just because we won that engagement did not mean that we had the luxury of taking our time. Even the comparatively soft shots of the pint size SMG would have echoed loud enough off of the hills to be heard by nearby duos, either from Atlantis behind us or any other nearby town we had yet to visit. That included The Spot up ahead.

I opted to loot the shotgunner, both because he was close and because the shotgun was my preferred weapon of choice. I played it loose and fast and that usually only worked out at close range, so a shotgun made sense. It was a pump action, too, complete with a speed loader and enough shells to get me started. Turns out Goemon planned ahead with his aim, and opted against any shots higher than chest level. The body armor in the loot crate was Swiss cheese, but the helmet shined like a brand new car. I decided to take it for a spin.

"Got any first aid or anything?" Goemon asked.

"I got some bandages, and a pump shotgun. And a level one helmet. You find anything good?"

"Heck yeah. I got an Uzi stock and extended mag. This baby's fully kitted."

The Uzi only held three attachments, so the goal of "fully kitting" it could be achieved with relative ease. It got even easier when another player found the gear for you, and then you just took it off their body. That being said, PBR either failed to disclose, or specifically chose not to, explain what the exact advantages gun modifications provided. The Uzi existed solely to dump as many bullets as quickly and in the smallest area possible, and the mods Goemon picked up would further that goal.

"We better move," Goemon said, and whether or not he saw something I did not I knew he was right.

3

The Spot

"Shouldn't we heal first? You, I mean. I'm golden," I said.

"That's probably a good idea, but not here."

"To the shack!"

We had already spent too much time playing sitting duck in the middle of the plain. At least we had a decent excuse. The first kill of the round, especially when it was both members of a duo that got taken down, was always in the running for sweetest. Sure, Goemon did the heavy lifting, but it was my elite battlefield strategy that made it all possible. Not to mention landing those crucial shots with the Revolver.

The shack provided cover from our unseen enemies to the south. I pretended to stand watch in the other direction, but the knowledge that my shotgun would be useless at any kind of range made it tough to take my job too seriously. The grass probably offered more protection than I could.

I tossed the bandages over to Goemon and he began fumbling with them. "Need a little help?"

"It's not my fault. The game is glitching out."

Bandages work great so long as you have the time to apply them and enough to get the job done. At the moment we had plenty of both. A first aid kit healed you almost to full and in only a couple of seconds. One bandage healed about an eighth of your total HP, and each one took a few seconds to apply. They did not work so great in the middle of a firefight, but worked well enough during hard-earned downtime. After all, we won our first engagement and had the fortune of landing inside the first phase of the Safety Circle- the survival zone of PBR, the element of the game that kept players from just camping in one spot, designated as an unassuming white circle on the map.

Sooner or later the Circle would shrink, effectively dooming everyone that ended up outside of it to a painful, fiery demise in the zone we knew colloquially as "The Blue Wall of Death." As far as we both knew the Circle placement was entirely random, the result of some unseen algorithm placed by the devs to almost always screw us over. The size of the Safety Circle shrank exponentially over the course of the round. During the drop phase, the entire First Island map is open for business. The first appearance of the Circle does not happen for at least a few minutes after landing. Although, neither Goemon nor I had ever kept track- we were always too busy looting and dodging bullets to notice the timer in the beginning. The first Circle rarely proved to be much of a problem unless it appeared on a corner of the map and half the surface area took a useless residence in the ocean.

But we did not have to worry about the unprejudiced will of the Circle until later. The great clock in the sky had a few more minutes to go before it shrank the playable area. For the moment, the only thing on our minds was getting some long range weaponry, and maybe whether any duos were currently staring at us from the woods.

"Alright, I'm good to go. You need any?" Goemon asked.

"Nah, I was too fast for that joker. By the way, you're welcome."

"For what?"

"I let you have those kills. I could have taken them down with the pistol, but..."

"Oh, I bet."

"I just wanted you to get a confidence boost. It's important for the rest of the round."

"How bout you take the next one."

According to the map, a road cut through the hills and dead-ended at The Spot. The problem with roads is they get you where you want to go a little bit quicker but they also get you dead even quicker than that. Everyone playing the game looks for the poor saps lost enough, new enough, or both to just blindly follow the pavement. Plus, roads do more than just make you easy to spot. They conveniently leave out anywhere to hide, making anyone brazen or stupid enough to stay on one for long into a big, fat target.

We trekked up and over low, rolling hills. With no major settlements to explore on our chosen route, we stopped only to loot a couple of more shacks along the way. The shacks were nice enough to meet our low expectations, coughing up nothing but a smoke grenade and a grip modification for a rifle that neither of us owned. At least we found even less trouble along the way than we did loot.

In the distance a couple of naked trees and half of a chain link fence formed the boundary of The Spot. The town, if it could even be called that, consisted of two one story buildings, one three story, and one double decker as well as a low, wooden guard tower in the middle. There were other, smaller settlements or landmarks that had the honor of being given an actual written name on the map. For some reason The Spot did not make the cut and remained nameless and usually hidden to the masses. We labeled it The Spot both because of the reputation it developed in our playthroughs as "the spot" where the loot is often decent, and "the spot" we most often landed at when jumping out of the plane at the beginning of rounds. Because The Spot had no designated name on the map, and because it happened to be positioned in a relative dead zone, other players did not drop there much.

I could see only closed doors from my vantage point. That meant the place was untouched. Maybe I had the bad idea to land somewhere different at the start of the match, but things were looking up. We managed to get back to The Spot unscathed and the location itself was still untouched. I ran into the smaller of the one stories, and Goemon ran into the double decker just on the other side of a waist-high broken wall.

Looting turned into a mad dash like always. I felt like a fat kid at a cleared out buffet, grabbing anything still available but keeping an eye out for some hidden treasure overlooked by everyone else. A pistol and a few modifications sat on the lone table in the place. I equipped the silencer, more out of habit than actual necessity. A pistol silencer never made the difference between a win and a loss, but it did look cool. The M9 next to the gear held twice as many bullets than my Revolver but it packed less of a punch and was not worth the effort of swapping out the mods and the different kind of ammo. I checked on Goemon to see if he was faring any better.

"How you making out?"

"Level one helmet in here, level one vest...nothing good yet. You?"

"Tons of stuff. For a pistol."

"Not even worth picking it up...oh, and someone left a level two vest on top of this toilet. Must have been an intense trip to the bathroom."

A level two Kevlar vest functioned the same as its little brother but could soak up something like double the bullets. The extra protection weighed about twice as much as a result but it was well worth the price. Besides, the extra size gave you more storage slots as an added bonus. Gotta have somewhere to store all the gun mods that we would probably never get a chance to use.

After hearing Goemon's good news I checked the bathroom in my building. The door opened the same as all the others: way too loud. Every door in the entire First Island map rested on rusted out hinges, or at least sounded that way. This made it so that entering a building and shutting the door behind you to stop the cold air from running out was the sound equivalent of firing a flaregun into the air. Anyone close by would hear it, anyone upstairs in the same building would definitely hear it, and it became quite easy to tell if someone was coming or going just by the sound of creaky hinges and heavy footsteps. As a matter of fact, I could hear Goemon stomping around, opening and closing the doors of his building next door as clear as if he were in the same room as me.

"I found an AK," he shouted. A great find, and just what we needed. The AK-47 was the workhorse of the game. You could not upgrade it much- it accepted nothing but a new magazine, a scope or sight and something for the muzzle. The rifle boasted sheer firepower to make up for its slow rate of fire and bucking bronco kick. It worked fine at close range, able to tear through walls and vests with ease thanks to the 7.62mm rounds, especially since the recoil on the thing made it impossible to get off accurate bursts- anyone caught in a hallway staring down a fully automatic AK was going to have a bad time. Fortunately, the first bullet fired was so precise even at range that it could hold its own against other, more modern rifles provided you had enough self-control to fire one shot at a time. Goemon had that control, and I did not, so I was glad he was the one to pick it up.

My bathroom came up empty, so I turned around to inspect the kitchen one more time. Unfortunately, nothing new magically appeared in the ten seconds since I last checked it and I had no use for dirty dishes. There was just one more room in the place and I needed it to come up big. I busted open the door like there was some poor girl inside that needed rescuing, and then I saw her. She was right next to the bed, shining and pretty and surrounded by boxes and boxes of ammo that I unfortunately just realized I had no way to carry thanks to my lack of a backpack.

"Don't worry, I got an UMP." I picked it up and loaded it with one 25-round magazine. The rest of the ammo would have to wait until I found something suitable to carry it in. I slapped the red dot sight on top and a vertical grip that I picked up earlier- essentially just a fitted handlebar- under the barrel, so I could aim and control recoil more effectively. The UMP, pronounced ump by people that knew what they were doing and you-em-pee by troglodytes, worked pretty good as a stopgap weapon until you found the right rifle. It was head of the SMG class, able to be fully modded with sight, grip, barrel, and mag mods, and I was already halfway there.

Then, Goemon jumped out a window and shattered glass rained two stories down into the turf. Reflexes raised my UMP in the direction of the noise and I was embarrassed at my lack of cool. I needed to relax.

"You almost gave me a heart attack," Goemon said.

"What do you mean? You're the one jumping out these windows, all reckless. Throwing caution to the wind."

"Ha ha, very funny. Seriously though if anyone is remotely close by they definitely know we're here now."

"You didn't jump out that window?"

"No."

"Well it wasn't me. If it wasn't you then-"

"Wait, shh."

I froze in place and listened for any noise- some clue as to what was going on. I heard hard footsteps- coming from inside a building. "Stop moving," I whispered.

"I'm not. They're coming from next door."

4

Company

"Don't move. Maybe they don't know we're here," I whispered over the intercom. Goemon was one building over, and the separation between us might as well have been the river running through the whole map. Had it been later in the game, with a smaller Safety Circle and a smaller playing area, I would have employed the buddy system. I would have ensured if one of us went inside a building then we both did. But this was still the first phase of the round. We should have been all alone.

The footsteps ceased. I sat crouched in a kind of pretzel ball underneath the window facing the noise and considered the most opportune time to peek out. I wanted some trace of the intruders before I exposed my own hiding spot.

"They definitely know we're here," Goemon said. He was probably right, and they were doing the exact same thing we were: waiting for the enemy to move, to reload a magazine, or open a door, any of which might as well have been a flashing neon sign pointing out their exact location.

After a few long seconds I said: "Maybe they left. They did jump out the window."

"Maybe. I don't think so."

"I'm gonna have a look."

"Don't you do it."

I considered leading with the UMP but decided the barrel sticking out the front of the window was too much of a dead giveaway. It was not worth the risk, even if keeping the gun low meant it would take me an extra second or so to aim and shoot. I popped my head up to the window for a look.

The other duo, or half of it anyways, had planned on that. A few dozen bullets shredded the glass and cut my hair a little too short for my taste and I fell back onto the cold tile floor. I was ready to grab the bandages, but my health was fine. Guess it was a tough shot for them.

"Holy- are you still alive?" Goemon asked.

"Yep."

"Where?"

I checked the compass. "North. 15-ish? I dunno. In the next building over. You can't hear them?"

"My sound is jacked. It sounds like they're right next to me."

I stayed low and flat underneath the window to avoid losing my head. That did not stop the invaders from trying to take it off with another wave of rounds. The gunfire had some heft to it which led me to believe it probably belonged to an automatic rifle rather than an SMG. Probably they picked it up in that same building, just thirty seconds or so before I might have.

"That's because they are right next to you," I said.

"How hurt are you?" Goemon asked.

"I'm good, they missed me the first time and now I'm just hiding. I think they're just trying to scare me."

"How dare they try and take The Spot from us."

"How dare they!"

The next flurry came in the form of words rather than

bullets. "Come on out of there, we don't bite." The voice was soft and high. Years of experience should have told me it belonged to a siren, trying to lure me out of safety just so they could pump me full of lead. At the same time, the invitation just sounded so genuine. And what was PBR if not just a way to bring people together? Oh, right, it was a last man standing, fight to the death battle royale simulator.

"Looks like we got ourselves a Mexican standoff," I cried out the window, my voice not resonating as deep as I would have liked.

"What are you doing?" Goemon whispered over the intercom.

"I mean, they already know I'm in here anyways. Might as well talk to them."

After a moment, the spokesperson for their duo chimed in again. "No we don't. We have you pinned down."

"So," I said.

"You have to have guns on us, too. Or else it doesn't count as a standoff," she said.

"Oh really."

"Yes, really."

"Goemon, now!"

"What do you mean now?" Goemon said.

"I mean...shoot through the windows or something."

Goemon always played it tactical. At least, it seemed tactical compared to my own tendency to want to get things done as quickly as possible. In reality I think he just had better survival instincts than I did. In this game, surviving was not simple, but your chances got a lot better if you had some cover and a lot worse if you did not.

This time anyway he listened to me, even if his delay

messed up my dramatic timing by a few seconds. I heard the roar of the AK over more shattered glass. I waited until midway through the burst before I popped up and aimed the red dot sight through my window. I caught sight of one, really just a shoulder on the second floor, but by the time I fired it had disappeared behind the wall again. I asked Goemon if he hit them.

"Maybe once, but I didn't have much of a shot. You?"

"Nope, they're still up there though."

"Oh they're up there. And they know I'm here, now."

"Alright," I hollered out the window again. "Just throw your weapons out the window and we'll let you go. As a sign of, you know, good faith." They responded with silence, and then I could have sworn I heard something like an empty tin can dropping on the floor of their building. I gave it a second and asked again. "Well? What do you say?"

They sent their answer out the window. A care package shaped and colored like an olive, only about the size of a softball, traveled well past Goemon's building and exploded right outside of mine. The wall protected me, but my ears were toast and all I could hear were church bells. No way they could have actually sent the grenade through my window, right? That was as close as they could get.

Another voice spoke up, the second girl in the duo. "Sorry about that," she said. Her voice was like a mouse compared to the first. She sounded genuine, and her partner apparently did not like that.

"Dammit, Elly, how many times do I have to tell you not to apologize. She's not sorry," the presumed leader made it clear out the window again.

The one apparently known as Elly followed up with: "Right, I'm not sorry!"

"Little Town is ours! We always drop here."

If Goemon and I were in the same room, we would have scoffed at each other. Come to think of it, I figured I should probably work on getting the band back together. We stood a much better chance in close proximity- if one of us got knocked, the other could play medic and pick him up before he bled out. On the other hand, I could sneak out around the back of the building and have my own backside covered. I might be able to get a better angle on the enemy duo. Goemon read at least half my mind and said: "What the heck is Little Town? This is The Spot."

"Yeah, and The Spot belongs to us," I agreed.

"The Spot? That's a stupid name. Like I said before, we always drop here."

"Well you didn't drop here this time, or you'd be long gone," I countered. "You haven't even looted the whole place yet."

"Well, Nails wanted to try something different," Elly said.

"It doesn't matter when we got here. What matters is Little Town is ours!" The girl named Nails affirmed.

I crawled across the dirt-slicked tile floor of my little building and pushed open the door. No doubt they heard it, but I knew they could not see me from that angle inside their building. Even if they did get wild enough to lean out the window, Goemon had me covered. I slithered around to the back of the one story and knew I was safe for the moment. Crawling had a couple of advantages, like being quieter than stomping around and opening up more opportunities for cover, but man it made for slow moving.

"What are you doing?" Goemon asked.

"I'm flanking. Don't worry. Just hold them in there."

"Oh, great idea. This should go well."

I crawled along the back of the building to the half

broken wall that ran near the side of it. The wall would become the linchpin of my flanking strategy, a solid (enough) fortification from which I could launch my attack. I tried to reassure Goemon. "Don't worry, they don't even know I'm here."

Of course, he had good enough reason to doubt my plan. More than one round had ended prematurely thanks to my general refusal to accept the concept of patience. I often ran out guns blazing without even telling Goemon what my plan was at all. Usually it was because I lacked one. In this case, he would have to be happy with the fact that I let him know beforehand.

I peered through the red dot sight and saw one of them through the second floor window, facing towards Goemon. This gave me plenty of time to line up the first shot. I held my breath to cut the shakes out and, when I was satisfied with the results, fired my best attempt at a controlled burst. The first bullet sent my target's helmet flying. The recoil control of the UMP was spectacular and it did most of the work for me, so I landed the next couple of shots as well.

"I shot her helmet off," I yelled.

"Is she knocked?"

"No!" Elly yelled right back, brandishing her rifle out the window before she drilled a few holes in both the wall I stood behind and myself. Her gun was louder, bigger, and more powerful. Even though I scored the headshot the both of us were probably equally injured. I ducked behind the wall again and hoped they had no more grenades to hurl. In the meantime, I threw my own. Of course, I forgot to pull the pin so it didn't help the situation much.

"I'm in big trouble," I said to Goemon, "but I'm still standing. Well, technically sitting, but I'm not knocked. And as you heard, she ain't either."

"I thought you got a headshot."

"I did! Her helmet flew right off. I don't know how this

game works. Maybe it's the UMP, you have to shoot them like ten times or something."

Either Elly or Nails interrupted our conversation with a few more bullets. A couple chipped away at the wall and the rest of them kicked up the dirt in front of me. I was fortunate that they missed, but they succeeded in making clear my immediate situation. My health bar was low, and I figured I could only take a couple of more rounds before I got knocked. The girls were probably healing up nice and good in there, but I gave Goemon all of my bandages.

"You got any health?" I asked him.

"Uh...I got a first aid kit," he said.

"I could probably sneak back around, get inside your building, if you cover the front."

"We should probably go."

"What do you mean?"

"I mean look where the Circle is gonna end up. The Blue is going to kill you."

I watched another orb fly out the window. This time, I was fairly certain my time in PBR was over, and I was a moment away from a frag grenade exploding me straight out of the game, out of the cyber cafe, and into Super Mario World. Instead, it went off with just a flash and a whimper. I saw the great white light, but not because I was dead. I was just blind, and they had thrown a stun grenade rather than one of the explosive variety. Now, my entire world was nothing but white.

I took the news in stride. "Well, I'll never see again for the rest of my life."

Goemon was not concerned about my newfound lack of vision. "They're definitely running out the back. The Blue is coming in."

"Well, you could, you know, go after them. Or you could

be a true friend and heal me up before I burn to death."

5

Boundaries

Goemon wanted to go after the duo. We both knew that without the need for him to say anything. There was more than just winning the match in Project Battle Royale. Goemon judged his success by how high the number of kills was on the scoreboard at the end of the round. Whether he wanted to save me out of the kindness of his heart or simply because he did not want me to hassle him like a haunting ghost in spectator mode for the rest of the match did not really matter. He came to get me like a best friend would.

"We should have had them," Goemon said.

"Hey, I got a headshot. Softened them up. I figured maybe you could do the rest."

"Oh, I'm sorry," he said with extra drama just to prove that the apology was fake.

"Don't worry. They have to make it to The Circle just like we do. And it's far, so we'll both be headed that direction."

"Yeah, we'll probably see them. Here. Hurry up, we gotta go."

He tossed me a First Aid Kit- a heal good enough to refill 80 percent of your health in just a few seconds. In order to get back to full health, I would need to pound a couple of energy drinks, down a bottle of painkillers, or luck out on an adrenaline syringe. While I patched myself up, I watched the perimeter of the great cloudy wall we called the Blue march forward. The size of it, essentially the entirety of the map from our current perspective always made me doubt its speed. Only when you ran from the Blue did you get a real idea of how quick it moved.

I did not need the map to tell me we were in the wrong spot. The Blue Wall did a fine job of that. It enveloped us the moment I finished healing. Correction: it enveloped me, because Goemon had already taken off, sprinting in the opposite direction of the moving deathtrap. While inside the Blue, everything got hazy and just a little distorted, not unlike real life at 3:30 AM after a fourth can of Surge. Also similar to real life was the excruciating pain that resulted from merely existing in the wrong place at the wrong time. Being in the Blue was not a pleasant experience, and it only got worse as the round progressed. This being the first phase, the pain was only slightly worse than a throbbing headache or the embarrassment of going to the homecoming dance without a date.

My life bar flashed, too, as if I needed more of a reminder that I was getting hurt and I needed to move. I took off running after Goemon and decided to look at my map instead of the scenery. The Circle could have picked a worse spot- it was southeast, but landlocked. If we moved quick we could make it before The BWOD ground our health bars to dust.

"The Spot never has a car when we need one," Goemon said. He was right, of course. Every time we ended up at the center of the great Circle a car would be there waiting, useless. If we needed to skip town and head across the map, the game always planned ahead and removed all forms of nearby motorized transportation first.

"I don't know why you're complaining. I'm the one burning alive back here," I said as I chased after him. He only had a second or two on me but it was enough to keep him out of the encroaching wall of Blue.

"Just be glad I didn't leave you behind. You see any cars?"

"I see a motor... rock."

"A motor rock. Just what we need. Whatever, we'll make it without."

It took a few minutes of sprinting, but I managed to catch and break through the barrier of the Blue Wall. What passed for air was sweeter on the outside, and my vision returned to normal again. But, I could not stop to enjoy it with the threat still nipping at my heels. "At least you can outrun the first one," I said between strides.

"The real question is, where is that duo? They had to head this way. I definitely don't want to get shot in the back." Goemon always thought about the next threat, the unseen one. I preferred to focus on the one right in front of us, or in this case the one right behind us. For the moment that meant the moving Wall of Death. In its pursuit, it emitted a low, oscillating hum like an industrial box fan and I found it impossible to ignore.

"You hear that?" he asked.

"The sound of our imminent death? Yeah, and it's driving me crazy. I hate the Blue, it's the worst way to die."

"No, not that. Listen!"

There were always too many sounds going on in PBR. It seemed like listening skills mattered just as much, if not more, than eagle eye vision. I tried to focus on whatever Goemon referred to over the noise of our shoes stomping through the grass and the Blue droning on behind us. I caught the hint of it, a soft vibration from far off. It was getting louder and no longer just a distant whisper.

"Car?" I asked.

"Too high pitched, definitely a motorcycle. We should hide, I don't really want to get caught in a drive by," Goemon said.

"Or, we could take the motorcycle by force, and catch everyone else in a series of drive-bys of our own."

"Genius."

The motorcycle screamed like a demon as it crested the hill. Fortunately Goemon and I lurked outside of any collision course with the cycle. It made our chances of getting run over much worse, but also did the same for our chances of actually landing any shots. It was hard enough to shoot someone moving at a light trot thanks to lag and the janky PBR game engine. Put your target on a motorcycle and it becomes virtually impossible to hit the shot with any consistency.

This never stopped me from trying. All the running had bought Goemon and I a few seconds before the Blue caught up to us, so I turned and aimed through the red dot sight. I tracked the bike as it cruised past us, long enough for Goemon to take notice.

"Don't shoot! They didn't see us."

I was unconvinced. "Exactly. It's the girls from The Spot. I can tell by the matching purple jackets. Plus, one of them is missing a helmet."

"So? We'll get them later."

I decided not to answer him. I let loose with the UMP and watched the bullets tear into the tree trunks behind the motorcycle. The bike swerved. I could tell the maneuver was not the result of my own accuracy, judging by how far behind my bullets landed. The noise of the gunshots and the accompanying surprise must have been enough to drum up some fear, causing the evasive maneuver.

"Are you insane!" Goemon yelled.

"How did they not flip," I said, searching for some justification as to why I gave away our position. They got lucky. It would have been an instant death if they crashed at that speed. I would never receive credit for it, but that wouldn't stop us from grabbing the loot and the bike to boot.

"Did you hit them?"

"Well, not exactly."

I scoped in on the motorcycle again. It was hopelessly out of range. I had as much chance hitting it now as I did finishing school at the top of my class. The girl on the back of the bike, Elly, looked back. I would have been happy with just her smile. Unfortunately, she combined it with a gesture featuring one of her fingers. Although, who knows, they were pretty far away so it is possible she was just giving a flirtatious wave.

I watched the bike, and the only woman who ever truly loved me, disappear out of view. It was our first fight! We would remember that day forever, and laugh, and reminisce...if I ever saw her again. I could have sat there and contemplated for the rest of the night, only the game had different plans for me already.

The worst case scenario might have simply been getting run over by the motorcycle. It was as embarrassing a way to go as PBR had to offer. We dodged that one, so I figured being the optimist I would think of the second worst case scenario. Here's what I came up with: I blew my shot, alerted anyone in the tri-county area to our presence, and then a duo would set up shop in a town just inside the perimeter of the Circle, exactly where we were headed, guns trained on us long before we ever got the chance to see them.

Turns out I was half right. Someone did hear my pitiful assassination attempt. Fresh bullets flew at us, from where, I could not be sure. "Well, I hope it was worth it," Goemon said.

"I had the shot! I had to take it. And by it, I mean half a clip."

"Yeah, you did, and now this other duo's waiting for us and we've got nowhere to go."

"You sure they're in front of us?"

"Only thing I'm sure of is that we're screwed." He was poised, gun resting on the rock, looking for any signs of movement in front of us. I flipped around and looked behind us.

"They couldn't be shooting at us from in front. These guys are still in the Blue."

It was either luck or careful, strategic planning and game sense that caused Goemon and I to end up where we did. Obviously I would say the latter, but there was no time to think too deeply about it. I scanned the terrain behind us. A muzzle flashed bright through the haze of the approaching Blue menace. The perpetrator was leaned around the trunk of a tree, trying to make it so he would be a harder target to hit. He was successful on that front- it was tough to see anything other than his head and the barrel. Even with us out in the open, though, he only landed a shot or two to my vest.

"Behind us!" I called out. Then I remembered that Goemon hated that callout because it wasn't direct enough. "West, north west, kinda."

Even though the majority of our adversary was hidden behind a tree, the part of him that was sticking out became that much easier to focus on. Goemon spun around and aimed and we both fired on cue. I hit him for sure, but Goemon's AK delivered the final blow. The player fell to the ground, limp, and a loot crate appeared alongside him. The instant death meant he was a solo- a solo player does not end up in the downed phase, because there is no teammate to pick him up. No second chances if you have no teammate. That meant his partner was already long out of the round.

"Nice shot," I said.

"That guy was not very good," Goemon reloaded his AK with a fresh magazine, even though he only spent a few bullets.

"No, he wasn't, but he still got destroyed. Let's go loot him."

"Ah, I don't think we have enough time...we still have to get away from this Blue."

"But...it's like you just reeled in a trophy fish, and you're cutting the line."

"You're ridiculous. If we go loot that dude, we'll never make it back out. It doesn't matter what we find, because we'll be dead before we even get a chance to equip it."

As much as it pained me to leave that loot, especially when it was so close, I knew he was right. Even I wasn't reckless enough to charge headlong back into the boiling Blue sea just for some mystery rifle. Despite how the game sometimes played out, the entire goal of Project Battle Royale was to survive. The best gun in the game did nothing to stop you from drowning. I was just happy to be out of the first phase. We were off to a better start than we had been in weeks.

6

Resort
Last Week

Jungle Island rounds started off a bit different than the other maps. To be clear, the drop phase is the official start of a round no matter where you are. Once you take your seat in the cargo plane the only way off is with a parachute out the back. But technically the beginning starts a few minutes before the plane ride.

Players have to connect to the server first, and there has to be enough players in the server to even make it worth getting the plane off the ground. People from all over the world might end up in the same server and the same round. For this reason, PBR implemented a sort of interactive waiting room. Jungle Island featured a five star resort masquerading as such a room. What made it five stars? I don't actually know because I've never been to a five star resort but I can assume that this place was top of the line.

A floating poolside cantina bar marked the center of the resort. Lounge chairs surrounded it on each side in stadium-style rows. Then there was the pool, carved out of green stone like the rest of the entire place. It's possible the devs reused some assets from the Ancient Ruins to design the resort, but you had to hand it to them, the place was relaxing.

Activities included lounging on the copious reclined chairs, swimming in the fountain, or climbing on top of the hotel rooftop and launching into the pool. Everyone started with thirty apples in their inventory to throw at each other, but apple fights here were less about face contact and more who could throw the farthest. For whatever reason, players just seemed more at ease and less confrontational at the resort waiting room. You could even have an actual, decent conversation, something unheard of everywhere else in the entire game.

A man in a trench coat, hood, and bandana mask approached us in the pool. It was hands down the second worst pool party outfit I had ever seen, the first being when I had to borrow my dad's ancient parachute sized swim trunks and I got laughed off the beach a few summers ago. Anyways, in any other situation this random player would have thrown an apple in my face or insulted my discount store high tops. But, he did not yell, he did not quarrel, he did not demean. Instead, he talked.

"How was your day?" he asked. Such a simple, yet meaningful, and uncommon question.

"Uh, pretty good," I answered. "How was yours?"

"Good, brother, thanks a lot for asking. I just ate a monster burrito."

"What kind? Carnitas? Al pastor?" Goemon asked.

"Carne asada."

"Ah, a classic."

"Sometimes it's nice to not have to think about it, you know?" the stranger, or Sniffles, according to his name in the chat, said.

"That's true. Can't go wrong with carne asada," I said.

"But why not a California burrito?" Goemon asked.

"Oh, bro, I've heard of California burritos. But we don't have them up here," Sniffles said.

"Bummer. Where you at?"

"Washington. But that's OK, bro. I got my vape filled, got a cold drink. Life is good."

"You know, life is good," I added.

"Hey, good luck have fun bro," Sniffles said.

The final seconds of the round commencement timer ticked down. I thought about Sniffles and our lovely, positive interaction. These were people, real people, with dreams and wants and loves. They were not just targets in body armor, game for the hunting. I was more, too. Yeah, we had been on one heck of a losing streak. In fact, I could not remember the last time I got a decent frag. Maybe none of that mattered. At least, that was what the resort would massage into my brain.

Unfortunately, the resort was a stark contrast to the design of the rest of the map. See, Jungle Island is the smallest of the PBR maps. There was a bit of player backlash at the sheer size and emptiness of Desert Island, and the developers listened. Again they used a Para to swat a fly in their attempt at making positive changes, but technically it was a solution to the problem of "too big."

Using the First Island map as a reference point, they created something intended to be small and frantic, with no real empty sections of the map and no safety zones. The original map got chopped up in half and half again, then trimmed up and placed in something reminiscent of Southeast Asian jungle. Hence, the name Jungle Island- a tiny, deadly, and beautiful square.

This go around, we had entered the waiting room late. I had yet to get my fill of the resort's amenities. I had dreams of dropping there and becoming king of the hill. Then Goemon and I could relax poolside, sidle up to the bar and bask in the glory of all the loot and the majestic stone statues.

"Let's drop at The Resort," I told him.

"That place is a deathtrap," he responded.

"No, it's OK, I figured it out."

"Oh no."

"Come on, we never drop there anymore."

"For good reason. But fine."

As soon as the plane took off, the piercing rumble of the motor pushed any sense of calmness or peace out of my mind. Maybe that was why they made the noise so annoying. It was designed to amp you up, shake you loose from the shackles of some faux relaxation. This was not a pleasure cruise. This was war, apparently.

We leapt out of the back of the cargo drop plane as it crossed the resort. Approximately fifty other players did, too. It was more than I had expected, but my plan could still work. We would parachute just outside the wall, and sneak into one of the rooms through a window. There, we could hole up while the riffraff sorted itself out a bit. I explained the plan to Goemon.

"Good plan," he said, deadpan.

"Is it? I can't tell if you're being serious."

"I think it could work."

Our drop timing placed us squarely in the middle of the pack. Could have been better, could have been worse. But the plan could still work. I steered my parachute towards the south-western side of a corner wall, and I assumed Goemon would follow suit. When I landed he was nowhere to be found.

"Dude I thought you were following me," I said.

"I thought I was."

"Are you on the other side of the wall?"

"I guess so. Uh oh, there's someone here. He's coming after me. He's got this crazy look in his eye."

"I'll be right there."

Not like I had a weapon to bail him out with, but I figured

four fists were better than two. I sprinted alongside the wall. The turn was about fifteen feet in front of me. Then, I heard someone familiar shout to my left.

"Where you running to, bro," the voice called. It was dark and sinister. I looked ahead, to my left. A figure emerged from behind a dense patch of ferns and blocked my path. My heart sank. It was Sniffles. I noticed for the first time the fingerless gloves on his hands.

"I uh," I stumbled. "Goemon, I need your help!"

"Busy over here. This guy's trying to punch me to death. Ow, he punched me."

"Oh, what have we here," Sniffles said. A machete materialized in his gloved hand. He must have picked it up in the shrubbery, equipping it now for dramatic effect. It worked. I was scared.

"Easy, Sniffles. Remember what we had," I said.

"I'm here for one reason, bro. Killing you. And taking what you have."

"But what about our conversation?" I said, running backwards. I could not face him, not with just my bare fists. "Also, I don't have anything for you to take. Also, that's two reasons."

"One reason, bro," Sniffles said as he took a swing with the machete. It clinked against the stone wall. "Slice you up. Now get back here."

As I sprinted away from the immediate danger, a new threat behind me destroyed my escape route. Gunshots rang out. They were small caliber by the sound of it, but big enough to cut through my t-shirt just fine. The shooter had yet to notice me, instead working on someone else nearby. But it was only a matter of time.

"I punched him back!" Goemon yelled. "Oh, he's trying to do the super punch. Get away from me. Get back!"

Alright, I thought. Goemon was not going to run away. I had to stay and fight, too. Besides, I had forgotten about the super punch. It was some weird mechanic they included where if you got a running start and jumped into a punch it was an instant KO. I had never seen anyone land a punch like that in real life and in fact I had never landed one in PBR, either.

"OK, bro-chacho," I said. It sounded even worse out loud. "Let's dance."

I charged at Sniffles. He ran at me. I would need perfect timing to leap and punch before getting chopped in half.

"How many times do you have to punch someone," Goemon said.

"Just...once!" I shouted as I launched off my back foot and into the air. I flung my fist forward a millisecond before Sniffles began his swing of the machete. It was all I needed. While the weapon was raised over his head, I connected with a solid right hook to the jaw. Sniffles went down.

"Uh oh, it's not looking good. One more and I'm done," Goemon said. I just needed him to hold on one more minute while I grabbed the machete.

"Ah, bro, not cool," Sniffles said. Unfortunately, I could not commandeer his weapon until I knocked him out permanently. So I began to wail on him with my fists, like a primal great ape, lost in a rage in the middle of the jungle. It was a far cry from the dreams of the resort but cathartic in its own messed up way. The guy did try and kill me first, after all.

I never got the chance to finish the job. The pistoleer trailing behind me had gotten his first frag, and I turned out to be his second. I never even found out if he was the other half of Sniffles' duo. It did not matter either way, because the round was over.

7

The Ruins

The Blue Wall of Death slumbered once again, and phase two of the round had officially begun. True, it was only a matter of time before the Blue woke back up. However, making it into the relative safe zone of the Circle put my mind at ease for the immediate future. All I needed to do was heal.

With no town close enough to provide us cover, we used the tall grass and the perimeter of the Blue Death as a substitute. It would be near impossible for anyone to sneak up behind us. If they were still in the death zone, they would not have the time to be quiet and we would hear them running from a mile away. In front of us we could see in nearly every direction, so all in all it felt like a safe enough spot to take a breather. I pulled out the first aid kit and went to work.

"Not bad for the first phase," I said. I could see Goemon scanning the horizon. He refused to relax. "You ever think maybe we should be out there?"

"Out where?" he asked.

"Outside. Trying to sneak into, you know, parties and stuff. You know. IRL."

Goemon turned to look at me. The avatar of his face failed to register any emotion whatsoever. It was enough of an answer.

"Yeah, me neither," I said.

Despite the claim, we both thought about it sometimes. It was like another world out there, and one we had no desire to be a part of. So we sought refuge within the boundaries of the world of PBR. The game provided its own version of social interaction, as strange as it might be. But it's not like social interaction was normal at a house party or the Irish pub next door to our cyber cafe. The only thing we lacked was girls, but even we managed to meet some in the game just a couple towns over. I kept more than a sliver of hope alive that we would see them again.

PBR was not so straightforward itself. The game world hid a sordid history both in its depths and in plain sight. With no single player or story mode, players could only speculate about the history of the island maps. The environment of First Island read mostly Eastern bloc warzone. After all, guns, ammo, and military-grade body armor littered the place. Most of the architecture represented itself with the sort of industrial sameness that could only come from Communist urban progress. To be fair, neither Goemon nor I had seen much IRL outside of the tri-state area, so even that guess might not be the most accurate.

On top of that, the game did not exactly strive for unflinching realism. Sure, the guns shot mostly like real guns when the lag was OK. But flashy outfits, flat-billed hats, and leopard-print rifle sweaters known as skins had become a cash cow feature for the game. The result was players running around in matching tracksuits or purple parachute pants donning hot pink shotguns. It really took away from the grim atmosphere. But if it wasn't really a warzone or a party palace, then what was it? Perhaps it was somewhere in between. Maybe without the graphic tees and cutoff shorts, the First Island PBR map might have the feel of an evacuated island, one ravaged by some highly contagious disease or zombie outbreak. And the island held secrets.

One of those secrets was broken into pieces half buried

and spread throughout the field in front of us. The Ancient Ruins were enough to leave any player speechless upon seeing them for the first time, even in their decayed state. A perimeter of massive columns protruded from the ground at all angles like the bones of a broken ribcage. Great stone carvings filled the interior alongside the remnants of an archaeological outpost. It also held enough guns and ammunition to take down any would-be tomb raider.

"What do you think archaeologists need AK47s for?" I thought out loud. "Just what kind of archaeology is this?"

"I don't know, man," Goemon laughed, "Don't you think the devs just put this stuff in here to mix up the terrain?"

"How can you call these ancient ruins stuff? Where's your imagination? Your sense of adventure?"

"They're busy. We've got a round to win."

"Fine, but I'm just saying, I think the Ruins are clearly part of a bigger backstory."

"Hold up here," Goemon put a stop to our conversation and dropped into the tall grass. I followed suit. "Let's see if there's anyone inside."

We lacked the magnified scopes for a proper reconnaissance mission. However, the Ancient Ruins lacked any buildings to hide in which made spotting any foot traffic much easier. Plus, everything in those ruins shared the same sandy coloring. If a duo wearing some outlandish gear lurked within, we would know about it.

"See anything?" Goemon asked, his voice just barely above the wind.

"Nothing...wait. I saw movement."

"Movement?"

"Yeah, like a person. Or maybe just a leafy branch. It was only a second."

"Usually it's not a leafy branch."

"Well I'm not sure. You know how this game is." The game was partially responsible. My nerves took the rest of the blame. A twitching tree or a flapping bird out of the corner of your eye could drive you insane if tensions were high enough. And PBR always made sure tension was high enough.

This time it was not a leaf. I saw more movement out of the corner of my eye and snapped my focus to it. The silhouette stood out against the rock faces like blood in the snow. That meant at least one person had beat us to the Ruins. Judging by the guy's casual demeanor, his friend was probably close by. But we had the drop on them.

"There!" I called out.

"There where? Where is there?" Goemon asked.

"Uh. 60. You see him?"

"Oh I see him."

"Good, cause I'm gonna take the shot," I said.

"No. For the love of- with what? You'll never hit him. Just, no."

"Fine."

"Let's at least figure out where his buddy is."

"I can agree with that."

Goemon began to formulate an elaborate and presumably well thought out tactical strategy. Stay on the perimeter, he said. Something something element of surprise. Wind resistance, bullet drop, angles and geometry? I'm not positive. Important to make sure that we had a clear shot. Shoot when we could guarantee taking one of them down. I liked that part. My finger itched. He asked me if I was listening.

"Yeah, for sure. Let's do this."

Goemon was completely right about the element of surprise. Except in this case, in order to keep the enemy in the dark, I found it necessary to keep my partner guessing as well. He stuck with the plan of banking left, I think he said for a better angle or something? It didn't really matter, I had a plan of my own. I moved right, preparing to initiate a strategic flank and surprise attack. The time had come to get up close and personal.

I listened for footsteps over the pounding of my own and found them. The sound could have come from the other side of the wall, or it could have come from Australia. I really needed to work on my spatial awareness at some point. But not right now. At least I knew the general direction and felt confident enough the footsteps were close by.

The moment called for a battle cry but I suppressed the urge, keeping what remnant of secrecy I had left. Besides, I figured the shotgun could do enough roaring for me. My heart knew what was up and tried to either hightail it out of my chest or get first crack at the duo. Probably it was the former, but either way I tried to talk it into staying put. I filled my lungs with air a few times and tried my best to paint a picture in my head of the other side of the wall.

When I felt like I had as good of a mental image as I was going to get, I took one more big breath and leapt around the corner. My finger was already on the trigger and I fired from the hip as soon as I cleared the angle. Call it aim, good hearing or just plain luck but the bad guy was right where the shotgun and I expected him to be. A cloud of red mist flew into the air behind the buckshot, and as the other player turned around I lifted the gun up to eye level for a clearer shot. Goemon yelled something but I was too busy to make it out. I pumped and fired again, sending the player falling to the ground in confusion.

"One down!" I shouted in triumph. My target crawled behind a nearby wooden crate, just out of my range. No matter, he was neutralized anyways. Plus, I figured maybe he might lead us to his teammate.

"Holy- you are so far away from me. What the heck are you doing?" Goemon called back. He sounded less excited about my surprise plan as I would have hoped.

"I'm sure you heard. I just blasted one of them with the shotgun and he's down. Now, we just have to find his buddy." I kept my shotgun high and steady and moved quick towards the downed player. If I knew anything about playing duos in PBR, and I think I do, it's that the guy I shot's partner would be desperately trying to pick him up right around the corner, effectively giving me a free shot. I hurried around the crate. "He's probably right around this- oh no."

No way Goemon could have heard the last part of that sentence, but I know he got the gist of it judging by the crack of the gunshot that filled my ears and his comlink. He asked anyways. "Are you alive?"

"Alive, yes, barely, please get down here please please," I said. Funny how quick your confidence goes after you eat a sniper bullet. It had to be a sniper shot. The sound was loud enough and the damage matched to boot. The player I had so deftly shot gunned turned out to be just as good at crawling away, and I lost sight of him. Now I could not secure the kill and to make matters worse I had an angry sniper with some ideas about redecorating my helmet.

"I can't get an angle from here," Goemon said. "Just survive until I get down there."

I took a few more breaths in an attempt to steady the gun in my hands. It was not happening, but I did not care. Playing it easy was not what knocked down that player a few moments ago, no. I decided to let the adrenaline run through me. Besides, it's not like my current weapon of choice required perfect aim to be effective. I leaned around the crate, hoping to catch a glimpse of the sniper. He had yet to move. We both fired.

I probably hit him, but at that range the shotgun really let me down. It was definitely the gun's fault. Not mine. The sniper rifle, on the other hand, managed to hit me clean, and I fell to my knees. Fortunately for me I made it behind the crate again before he had a chance to chamber another round.

"Whelp, I'm dead. It's all over," I said, resigned to my fate. The panic left me and I felt, for the first time since we started playing, a sense of calm. Almost true peace knowing that the end was so close and that nothing could be done about it. "It's ok, go on without me. I'm…happy, now. I see the light."

"You're not dead," Goemon snapped me out of it. "You've got like 30 seconds left. Just don't get shot again and tell me where they are."

He was right. No need to give up so soon. "Alright. The first guy I knocked is somewhere over here, east of me. And I can hear the sniper running to pick him up."

"Alright. Just try and hide."

Hiding was not my favorite thing to do, but being incapacitated and all I figured I would take the advice. I crawled like a slug away from the footsteps behind me, and weaved through the maze of stone and crate to try and buy myself enough space to survive.

8

I Require Medical Assistance

My life was in Goemon's hands now. Probably it had been since the beginning of the round. Probably it had been for far longer than that. It just seemed far more true in my current state, being that I was downed, knocked, bleeding out, mortally wounded, or just generally messed up. If the game had a designated term for my condition it was out of my scope of knowledge. What I did know was that I had a minute or less before my life bar ticked down to oblivion. In that time, Goemon needed to finish off one wounded player, take down his most-likely-still-full-health buddy, and then sprint over to pick me up, and if he failed at either of those tasks the round was over.

"He's got a sniper rifle. Probably a K98 bolt action. You can take him if you get in close. Get aggressive, you know. Confidence, buddy."

"Good to know," he said.

I had a decent view of the incoming Goemon, but rows of crates and walls obscured any sight of the enemy. He crept forward with near silent footsteps. The enemy duo broke the tension, but not with the blast of a sniper rifle. Instead, something small and angry and fully automatic spewed out a bunch of bullets in his direction. He dove for cover.

"What the heck, man. You said sniper rifle. As in, one bullet at a time," Goemon said.

"He must've picked up his buddy I guess."

"Great, now I gotta take them both out?"

"Yeah, and could you pick up the pace a little? I'm dying over here."

"Alright, forget this."

Goemon popped out of cover the instant the bullets stopped coming. Although I could not see it happen firsthand, the scoreboard let me know he knocked his target out. "Nice," I said, playing cheerleader from the sideline. "That was the guy I downed already. They must not have any first aid."

The thunderclap of the sniper rifle sounded off again, but Goemon still had plenty of ammo left to respond. I looked back and forth between the scoreboard and my partner to piece together the action. Both players in the enemy duo were eliminated. Goemon did it, and not a moment too soon. I only had a few seconds left before I was toast myself. He trotted over to pick me up as if he had all the time in the world.

"See? I had a plan the whole time," I said as he knelt to pick me up. The timer began, and after a few seconds I would be able to walk around and shoot like normal again. Unless I healed up, though, one more bullet would send me right back to the ground.

"We got lucky," Goemon replied.

"Luck? That was all skill, those guys sucked."

"That's why we got lucky! If they were better we would have died for sure."

I got to my feet and brushed myself off. "Only have to be better than the guys we're fighting. Ever heard the one about the two friends camping and Bigfoot?"

"No."

"So, two best friends are camping. Late at night, they

hear some commotion outside of the tent. Cans getting knocked over, bags ripping, tree branches snapping, that type of thing. Possibly heavy breathing, and then a deep, animalistic rumble."

"That's Bigfoot?"

"Yeah, they determine it's a sasquatch. For sure, they've never been so sure of anything in their lives. So friend one says, we gotta get out of here. Friend two agrees. Friend one unzips the tent and as he's leaving, he turns back to check on his buddy. 'What are you doing?' he says. Friend two is on one knee, lacing up some running shoes. He continues: 'What, you think you're going to outrun that thing?' Friend two looks at him and says, 'I don't have to outrun Bigfoot.'"

"What in the world kind of a story is that? Are you trying to say you're going to use me as bait? Why Bigfoot?"

"No, not you. We're both the guy with the shoes. Trying to, you know, outrun- outlast- the other team. Against an unknown enemy. What do you think?"

"I think you've lost it." Goemon knelt by what was left of the sniper rifle-wielding player. I should have bet money on it. Every round, no matter the circumstance, sooner or later he ended up with a sniper rifle. "Looks like this guy had a Kar. With a three by scope, too." The click of a fresh magazine made it clear there was ammo to spare. The Kar might have been old school- it was made from wood and fired only a shot at a time, requiring the bolt to be pulled back before every squeeze of the trigger. But it turns out anything that shoots a piece of lead straight and fast and a full kilometer away is still pretty good in a fight.

I checked the other player's pack. No usable health to speak of, and I would have settled for a ripped bandage and half a can of soda. The guy's vest had soaked up its last bullet, but his level one helmet would do nicely. Sometimes being a bad shot had its perks. He also wielded a semi-automatic Mini-14 rifle which I raised to the sky in triumph. It was a personal favorite of mine, with the accuracy of a sniper rifle and the flexibility of a much higher fire rate. It worked pretty good at a distance, too, which is exactly what I needed next to my trusty shotgun.

"I got a Mini. And a two times scope. And...a level three backpack," I shouted.

The level three backpack had enough room to fit roughly two of everything, kind of like the Arc. It was an excess of space considering my current humble loadout but at least I would not have to worry about running out of room for the rest of the match.

"Dude nice. Did you get a new helmet?" Goemon said.

"Yeah, but my vest and the corpse's are shredded. Also, no first aid kits."

"I have...two bandages for you."

Goemon tossed them over. Not even enough to get me back up to half health. It did cease the blurred vision, so that was a big positive.

"There's never any health at the Ruins," I said.

"Nope."

"We've got to go somewhere to get some more useful loot."

"Yep."

"I mean, we've got good guns now, right?"

"Mhm."

"So we should be fine if we hit Big City," I said, checking the map. It was the closest place with guaranteed health. Big City boasted enough variety of buildings to guarantee some of everything.

"Sure."

"We're going to die there, aren't we."

"Absolutely."

"Well, I'm going to be dead either way if I don't patch up these potholes in my guts. Might as well go out with a bang. Actually, I don't want to explode again. I hate that."

"Can't argue with that. I'm following you."

Dropping in a city at the start of the match was a death sentence. Not one of those sit-on-death-row-for-twenty-years sentences, either. No, execution by firing squad was usually carried out within the first minute of the round. By now we had been in the game for way longer than that.

The initial riot should have died down already. Big City would not be empty, though. Most of the looters would be dead, sure, but the strong that survived would be waiting to pick off the scavengers. Maybe scavengers is the wrong word. A little too harsh. I preferred to think of us more as prospectors. Opportunists.

As we crept along the outskirts of the place, the damage became apparent. Corpses and their abandoned loot boxes dotted the landscape like a Walmart after Black Friday. Combined with the dilapidated architecture of the Soviet-era apartment buildings, the shattered windows and the open front doors, it looked like a plague tornado plowed through the place. Of course, I knew better.

"The greatest natural disaster," I ruminated.

"What?"

"Man. See what I did there? Man is the greatest-"

"Shh," Goemon cut me off.

Silence permeated the place, like it did in the inside of my car that time I gave Samantha a ride home after sixth period. Our footsteps, on the other hand, grew louder by comparison. I was bright enough to understand why Goemon wanted me to shut my trap. The time for listening had come. Footsteps would be just as good as alarm bells at giving us a heads up.

A chunk missing from the cinder block perimeter wall allowed us to climb through without having to scale the thing. Vaulting over the top did not make as much noise as crashing through a window but it was close. Fortunately we just climbed on in to Big City's limits. It should also be noted that the city was not called Big City. We christened the place Big City from the very first time we played the map and it stuck around. The actual name was unpronounceable by any tongue residing within several thousand miles. It sounded like a brand that belonged on a pickled root vegetable jar in the foreign foods section of the discount grocery mart.

The Hospital stood at the outskirts of the city which worked in our favor. It was, unfortunately, on the other side of the street, which did not. The only thing between me and a full health bar was two lanes of asphalt and a half dozen bodies. The front door would be unlocked. They always were.

There was also the fear of what lurked at the end of said street. Crossing it would leave us completely without cover. However, if someone shot at us it meant they were so bored after looting the town that they had nothing better to do than stick their rifle out the window. It was possible, but this was the second worst kind of player. The worst offender would be too scared to even stick the rifle out the window and instead just wait behind a door inside the building, for minutes or hours, until someone turned the knob and they could go bang. In either case, I figured I needed the health badly enough to take the chance.

I led the way, of course. As designated trailblazer, crossing the street first was my duty. Goemon watched my back as I sprinted across what might as well have been a bed of coals.

"Wait, what are you doing?" Goemon whisper shouted at me.

"Am I clear?" I asked back. The lure of the loot was

too great. Everybody knows you get the best stuff from other players. And there were so many other eliminated players here!

"You're in the middle of the street. I can't see in the windows."

"Just cover me."

"Oh, OK, sure."

"Ah, nothing good. Just a dinosaur mask and a machete."

I figured it was worth a glance at one box. Yeah, it came up empty, but the unknown would forever haunt me more than getting gunned down in the middle of the street.

"Then get inside already!" Goemon shouted, staring through the scope of his rifle down the still-empty street.

"I'm just waiting on you."

I had the door to the hospital open and the hallway cleared by the time he made it across.

The doors inside and out remained closed before our entry, usually a telltale sign the place had yet to be looted. But the inside of the place looked as rough as the outside. Rusted gurneys and medical supplies scattered around the hallways gave the impression it had been cleaned out, but the few flickering fluorescent lamps provided less than enough light to make out what actually happened in there. I think I saw a bullet hole or 20 and the sterile smell of a normal medical center mixed with gunpowder only increased my suspicions.

This time, I chose to keep quiet and play the listening game on my own. If there was someone in there with us they would know first. Footsteps outside only amped my pulse. Turns out they were Goemon's, but I stayed jumpy. He resealed the metal door behind him, and what was left of the sunshine disappeared behind it.

9

Out of Network Provider

The Mini rifle, while great at a distance, struggled indoors. Fortunately, the shotgun I had equipped was more than capable of clearing out a room. As the light continued to flicker, my hands went white from the strength of my grip on the gun. There would be no aiming if someone lurked around the corner. Only shooting. Gods have mercy on Goemon's soul if he so much as sneezed.

Yet behind every privacy curtain and inside of every patient room, the only thing to be found was bandages and useless medical tools. No bad guys lurked around any corner. I can't say I blamed them. The building was dark and dead.

"This place gives me the creeps," Goemon said.

"Me too. You find anything yet?"

"Just some bandages. I was holding out for a first aid kit for you."

"That would be nice."

"Ah!" Goemon shouted and I pulled the trigger on my shotgun, blowing a hole in the wall in front of me. Lucky for him he was in the room across the hall.

"What? What?" I called.

"What? You shot! Who are you shooting at?"

"You scared me. I'm shooting at no one. I'm shooting at a

wall. That's just how scared I am."

"Sorry. I just saw a weird shadow."

"Let's get the health and get out of here." Speaking of which, I thought I saw some in the next room through the hole I put in the wall.

"Yeah, well they definitely know we're here now," Goemon said.

"Yeah, well maybe you shouldn't have scared me."

"Are you done?"

"Yes. Hey, a medkit!"

I picked up the medkit and initiated the healing process. It was best to have your partner watch your back while you healed but I could not resist. I figured I would find some first aid but the medkit score was like getting a bonus curly fry in with your regular fry order. Even first aid only got you to three quarters health without the aid of pain pills or some other boost. After a few long seconds, the medkit took me right up to the top, full health and a new lease on life.

"Feel better?" Goemon said from the doorway.

"Feelin' fine," I said.

"Good, cause I think I heard someone break a window or something down the street."

"What's the play? Stay here and hide? Go out guns blazing?"

"No good angles in here."

"Mm."

"Next door is four stories and a roof."

"Vantage point."

"Exactly."

"After you."

Our destination was close enough to keep us unexposed among the cover of the surrounding towers. When advancing from building to building in the maze of Big City, I always felt a bit like a couple of mice scurrying from one hole in the wall to the next. Just had to hope no one had a trap set up for us when we got there. From the sound of it the reigning kings of the hill occupied themselves at least a block away. That put our chances at surviving relocation at "decent." It was hard to get better odds than that in this game.

Big City was a town of the Eastern bloc. Dozens of identical, functional, and seemingly efficient structures rose up between four and five stories around every street. The only thing more drab and gray then the tons of cinderblock that comprised the place was the perpetual desaturated haze that lingered over the sky. Maybe it was fallout or maybe it was just fog, but the game never made it quite clear. In either case, the sun was unwelcome. It was like downtown Portland made out of gray building blocks and without the variety of street food.

Despite the security bars fixed to the ground level windows, the front door remained open. I made sure to shut it behind us on the way in. The sound of the door opening worked about as good as an Acme booby trap. Even if you heard footsteps coming, you knew the enemy was not inside the house until that door creaked open.

The lower floor had been picked through already, save for some boxes of 9mm ammo and junk pistol mods. At this stage in the round, stopping to pick up an extended mag mod for a pea shooter just made no sense. I glanced in the kitchen just in case. Nothing good, so I followed Goemon up the stairs.

The corners looked clear. Meanwhile, Goemon had already selected a sniper's window. The barrel of the Kar sniper rifle must have been a dead giveaway to anyone watching outside. Probably it was better to bet on taking the first shot rather than hiding in the corner.

"I see one," Goemon said. "Seventy...five. Not coming this way. Heading right."

"I wanna see." I picked a nearby spot and switched back to my rifle. The only view the window offered was more crumbling apartments, and maybe a grocery shop of some kind with a rolling security door stuck half open. No players, though. "I don't see him."

"He ran inside," Goemon replied.

"Where?"

"The gray building."

"The one with the garage?"

"The gray one."

"They're all gray," I said.

"That one's red."

"But he's not in that one, right?"

"No."

"Where's his buddy?"

"I didn't see him."

"Do they know we're here?"

"I don't think-" Goemon dropped to the floor. "Yes," he finished, just in time, too, because the swarm of gunfire that now attacked the ceiling would have done a number on his helmet and possibly the round bony part underneath.

"You should have shot him!" I pleaded.

"You're right, what was I thinking," he scoffed. "I think it was the guy I spotted. Some kind of AR probably. Can you see him?"

"No, he's on the other side of the building. I'm going to try and peek him. I need a good angle."

"Don't you do it."

But it was too late. I was compelled to do it. It was my job to do it. My duty, my sole purpose. I couldn't just let some joker out there get away with firing in our general direction. He would think twice about shooting at us again. Actually he would not think twice because he would be dead. Because I shot him! Oh yeah, that's good.

While Goemon crawled away to safety, I took aim out the window. I started several feet back from the edge to maximize the defensive angle. PBR was all about the angles game, see. You want to see your opponent without them seeing you. Even if you have to contort your body around so you can lean in just like so, head safely out of harm's way, Mini rifle aimed and...nothing to shoot at. Unless the other guy decided to climb up to the second level, being that far back offered no shot.

On the bright side my own head contained no new holes in it so he had no line of sight, either. How to proceed? I could step up to the window which was the obvious choice, I just had to score a headshot first. No problem since I knew right where he was. I put my finger on the trigger and worked on breath control.

"Wait," Goemon said. It broke my concentration.

"What. I was about to kill him."

"Let's go up another level."

"Ah, element of surprise."

"Yeah plus then we can shoot down on him."

"I'm convinced."

"OK go slow."

We shuffled along the debris-strewn floor. Somehow we had transitioned from lab maze mouse to humble cockroach. Anything to stay alive, I guess, and sometimes that just meant keeping quiet. The silent slither strategy continued all the way up the stairs to the third floor.

Upon arrival the unmistakable sound of the front door opening echoed up the cement stairwell. We closed the door to our level, too, which the intruder downstairs may have heard, but would likely be unable to determine what floor we resided on. The next question became whether it was the guy we already spotted outside, come knocking for a closer look, or his mystery duo partner. Goemon read my mind.

"Stay away from the window," he whispered. "They don't know exactly where we are. I think it's the guy's buddy downstairs."

"So the first guy is still out there."

"I mean I don't know. I think so. Probably."

"That is great news. I've been dying to fire this thing. Wait, not dying. Itching. Yeah, that's better."

"Oh boy."

I raised up from prone to knee level, careful not to disturb a loose floor tile or so much as creak a board. Goemon, perhaps realizing he could not stop me, rolled so that he faced the sole entrance of our room. So far so good. Beyond the door lay the banister and stairwell. It would be a tough shot for both of us, mine out the window and my partner's at the enemy potentially peeking up the stairs. If he missed, we would be sitting ducks at that range. If I missed- ah, didn't matter, no point thinking about it, I wouldn't miss, so long as I could see him.

The glass of the window frame had been shattered long ago. I inched closer towards it. If the guy on the first floor had not been running around opening and closing doors so much, he probably could have heard the hollow-sounding movements of my boot on the wood. Instead, it gave me enough time to slide into position for the shot.

The sound from below stopped altogether as I scanned for the player outside. No signs of movement out there, either. The other duo was trying to wait us out, force us to make the first mistake. I hated this part, especially because for all my mastery of tactics I never could figure out if we had the advantage in a situation like this. Our room was secure in that we had eyes and a gun on the only way in. But if a grenade got tossed in there with us, game over. Even without the potential explosive, anyone holed up inside a building would have to leave eventually due to the encroachment of the Blue.

A glimmer of sunlight caught my eye from around a corner in the alleyway, maybe from a scope, maybe from a pair of ski goggles. It did not matter, because they belonged to the initial target. The shot was by no means clean, but the other player remained stationary, and he was looking away from me. To take said shot, I would need to march up closer to the window for a clear line. Even from my obscured position, I could tell the shooter was focused on another window- maybe even a different floor altogether.

"I don't think he knows we're up this high," I whispered, moving closer to the edge.

"Yeah? That's good, but I'm worried about this guy downstairs. What's he planning?"

"Dunno but he's about to be solo."

The sights of the Mini trembled just a bit until a breath hold steadied them. When they lined up with the helmet jutting out from around the corner of the building across the alley, I pulled the trigger and the crack of the rifle tore around our tiny room. A fine mist of blood dissipated in the air, but the helmet stayed put. I landed a shot, but missed the kill. Meanwhile, the player inside on presumably the bottom floor began a heavy sprint up the stairwell. He must have zeroed in on our location from the sound of gunfire.

"Uh oh. Upstairs?" Goemon said, standing up and heading out the door without waiting for my answer.

"Let's go," I replied anyway, chasing after him. The sound

of two duos' footsteps echoing around in the same vicinity would confuse things for everyone involved. All I could tell from the noise was that the guy downstairs was coming upstairs and the guy outside was heading closer.

"Did you get him?"

"Yes. No. Kind of. I shot him. He's still alive."

"Oh no."

"But definitely hurt."

"What happened?"

"I freaked out, OK? My crosshair was on his head. Maybe I needed to aim up to compensate. Or down. I don't know how shooting in this game works."

We barged into the fourth and final floor of the building and it was empty as expected. Goemon picked a corner and took a knee, looking towards the entryway. I chose the opposite and did the same, both of us ready to listen to the commotion best we could.

It did not take long for the telltale clink-clink of a metal grenade bouncing around an apartment floor to make an appearance. I somehow did not die of a heart attack, so I took the opportunity to look around the room in search of the noise.

"Was that...beneath us?" Goemon asked.

"I don't see anything."

The footsteps, now indeed directly beneath us, also became clearer. That is, they did for a second or two before my eardrums shattered. The grenade exploded, taking my sense of hearing with it and probably the dishes left molding in the sink of the kitchen one floor below. It did not stop there.

"Holy-" Goemon started.

"What, what?" I asked.

"Look at the scoreboard. BassMan, teamkill, grenade, KK-

KatFish."

"Oh no."

"Oh yes!"

"He killed his buddy? With a grenade? Through the window?"

"Yes!"

"Incredible. Fantastic. The best, absolutely amazing."

"Yes."

"We played it perfectly."

"We did. But we still have to take out the other guy."

"Or do we?" I asked, as another timely message scrolled by. Bassman disconnected (Reason: user left match).

"He rage quit!" Goemon exclaimed.

"He couldn't handle the shame," I laughed. To be fair, I did not blame him.

10

Desert Island
Two Weeks Ago

Desert Island might have been Texas. It might have been Mexico. Both of those places were much larger and probably shared the common trait of having distinct and varied topography. But I have not been to Texas and I have not been to Mexico and I am quite certain that the developers had yet to visit those places either when they made the game. Desert Island shared the classic film interpretation of Mexico and its neighbor Texas. The color palette consisted of brown, tan, café, and a smattering of beige. The sky was blue when it was not obscured by a swirling cloud of sand.

Rocks of all the sizes between pebble and boulder held fast in the wind. The paved streets needed work and the dirt roads only differentiated themselves from the surrounding terrain by the occasional tire track. Plant life had never existed there, which begged the question of where exactly the tumbleweeds rolled in from. Well, once I saw a cactus.

Desert Island was not the name of the map. The name was fake Spanish, something like Isladesierte or some other nonsense word the devs made up. We just called it that to differentiate it from the other maps. They were all islands, but this was the only desert. At least it was the only one until they released

Desert Island 2 but that map is a different story.

A large part of the appeal of PBR was the initial size of the play area. The breadth coupled with the skydiving mechanic created a unique freedom of choice in how to proceed with exploration. It wasn't free forever, with the moving Safety Circle and Blue Wall of Death eventually dictating where players had to go to survive. However, traversing the game's map- for all of its difficulty- provided an experience that was hard to match in other, more straightforward, deathmatch games.

When the devs created Desert Island, they took the original Eastern Bloc First Island map and doubled it. Naturally with all that space to explore, Goemon and I dropped in the same spot every time. The sandy little town was called Picante and we called its outskirts home.

The size of the map sounded good in theory. Twice as much of a good thing, how can it be bad? Well for starters, getting stuck in the middle of nowhere is the worst part of the game. The entirety of Desert Island is the middle of nowhere. But landmarks do exist. There's a church and a graveyard, a sad western town or ten, and a drug kingpin's compound of some kind, and at least there are more vehicles to hopefully get you from point A to point B because if you fail to get one you just die from the elements of the barren wasteland. The giant, dusty, empty Tex-Mex wasteland.

The cargo drop plane cut a precise diagonal path across the scorched earth, like a pizza knife slicing through a steaming thin crust pie. The flight path made me hungry for vengeance. I needed a win soon, but I could settle for a humane end to the current dry spell of frags. Pizza also would have been fine, but we ordered out yesterday.

"We gotta get something going here," I groaned over the sound of the roaring engine.

"I know. I don't know how much more of this I can take." Goemon said.

"We need to stick together, I think."

"Probably."

"Should we drop somewhere else?"

"Absolutely not."

We leapt out of the hatch of the plane. Spy movie physics applied during the drop phase. If you pointed your body straight and perpendicular to the ground while plummeting from the sky, you fell much faster. It was something akin to a screaming hawk cutting through the wind to catch a ground squirrel. You must fall faster to get to the ground first, to get to the weapons first, especially on a crowded flight path like this. To reiterate, shoot like a bullet towards the ground to get the guns to shoot the bullets.

By the time we pulled parachutes we could see about a dozen other players that had dropped with us. Parachutes opened everywhere, great buzzards in the distance circling the air, waiting to hit the ground to scavenge what they could. It would have been cause for major concern, except for the fact they all appeared to be aiming for the city center. Our target was located a couple minutes' walk outside the fenceless perimeter. It more or less passed for a suburb in the context of the rest of the map.

An empty sheet metal warehouse or industrial barn leaned into the dirt on the edge of the town of Picante. There was not enough graphical detail on the inside or the outside to discern it. The place had been inoperable for possibly ever. It lacked machinery, or an office, or barn doors, but it did have great loot to go along with the wooden beams that held up the structure. I always started there before working my way over to the heart of the suburb, all of five houses sitting in a circle like trail wagons round up for safety. This time around I found a backpack, a helmet, and a vest right off the bat. There was plenty more around the empty hall. I always wondered why everyone dropped into the city instead of the well-stocked outskirts.

After a couple more minutes of looking around corners I nabbed a Vector SMG. It boasted more upgrade slots than any other SMG and only lagged behind in the number of bullets it held. I hoped Goemon had made out as well as I had.

"What do you got?" I yelled as I left the rusty ware-barn-house and headed to the house circle.

"SCAR. You need anything?"

"I'm pretty much good to go. We should head over there, try and get there early."

"Sounds good."

We would be a bit late to the initial party, but if we hustled we could still get there on the tail end of the commotion. We had found decent weapons. All we needed now were a few decent, early kills. I was tired of dropping out of the plane, hunting for gear and never getting the chance to use it.

I poked my head in one casita and grabbed a first aid kit and a cool grip for my SMG. This must have been some kind of record for looting. That was good, because the actual town of Picante just a rifle shot away already sounded like a warzone.

The two main attractions of the city were a casino called Casino and some kind of indoor basketball/wrestling stadium. Both were deathtraps and we avoided them until most of the riffraff got sorted out. Several hotels dotted the city, and their hundreds of identical square windows could all potentially hold snipers once the round had continued long enough for everything to get settled.

I jogged down the half-paved road, past the highway sign riddled with bullet holes. To the left, a series of rock plateaus rose into the clear sky. To the right lay nothing but miles of desert. The road between our Spot #2 and Picante always ended up being one of the safer walks in the game. There were no weapons to pick up anywhere but the city or the place we landed at, which meant the chances of ambush stayed low. It was always nice to know the only threat lingered out in front rather than from behind a nearby boulder.

The domed wrestling basketball gym stood just beyond the city limits. Anybody upstairs there would have no angle on me. I turned around when I arrived at the first grouping of houses within the boundary of the city, mostly to see what else Goemon had looted. Only my partner in crime was nowhere to be found. The only friend there was the lonesome and dusty road.

"Hey, where are you?" I called into the voice chat.

"What do you mean? I'm in here. Where are you?" Goemon asked.

"I'm at Picante, at the houses."

"Oh no."

"I thought we were running over here!"

"There were still two more houses to loot. I found a scope. And an extended mag. And a shotgun."

"Yeah but speed!"

"OK, OK, I'll come over there."

The doors of every house near me had been left open. That meant the places had all been cleaned out. It also meant that some unknown number of enemy players could occupy the very same dwellings. I crouched with my back against the red stone slope. Keep the threat in front of me, I figured.

The warzone raged all around me. It rattled like a sound check for a melodic death metal band. The double bass drum sounds fine, you guys can take it easy now, I thought. Still, at least there was some distance between myself and that noise. I just needed Goemon to get to me.

"Five seconds," he said.

"Five seconds until you get here? I don't see you." There was nothing on that highway but empty promises.

"Oh sorry. Five seconds until I leave. Just don't die."

As he finished his sentiment, a face appeared in the window of the two story adobe house nearest me. Five seconds on the biggest map in the game proved far too long a time to wait. I was on my own, nothing more than a cutout paper target in a western shooting gallery. We should have stayed together.

The face belonged to the reaper, or maybe el diablo. Either way they had come for my soul. He knew exactly where I was, either from my chattering or my footsteps. I aimed the Vector SMG from the hip and fired. The glass shattered. I think the shot was good, but their shot was too and they must have hit me with something bigger. My helmet flew off and I hit the ground before it did. I swear I hit the shot. I swear I did not miss. But the other guy just stared at me through the broken window, holding my fate in his hands, able to finish it with one more pull of the trigger.

"I'm down," I said, dejected. Goemon could never reach me in time. Besides, I had no hole to crawl into. The only reason I was even still breathing was so the enemy player might get a chance to find out where my partner was hanging out.

"Ah man you gotta be kidding me," Goemon said.

"I shot him in the face. I know I did. I'm positive."

"I'm coming over there."

It was too late and he probably knew it, too, but there was no backup plan and nowhere else to go. I was stuck between a literal rock wall and a high powered firearm hammer. I was embarrassed and ashamed, crawling around like a wounded rat. As for Goemon, it was a march to his own execution. Sure, there was the slimmest chance of successful revenge. This alone motivated him forward. I mean, it was either that or give up and disconnect and we never disconnected.

I never caught sight of the second member of the duo. Goemon smashed through a bottom floor window. The sound of the footsteps switched from boot on tile to boot on wood. He was headed upstairs, brazen, unhinged, gun blazing. If he had stopped to pick me up we both would have died in a much more humiliating fashion.

It was over in about a second. The other duo knew he was up there and they were waiting for him. Maybe it was just the one guy, I never even found out. But el diablo got the drop on him and that's all it took. All of that time looting, the weapon mods, the parachuting, the optimism, the anticipation, all just a dirt devil that kicked up for a moment before dying back to the silent desert earth.

"How many times do you have to shoot somebody in this game?" my teammate yelled. I watched from the third person perspective as my lifeless course slumped over with no fanfare. My point of view spiraled into oblivion. He was dead and so was I and the round was over.

"We should have stayed together," I said.

11

Road Trippin

The first guy ended up with quite the haul after his loot of the place combined with all the players that went down before him. How nice of him to gather it all for us. There were enough bandages, first aid kits, and cans of mystery soda to keep us healed up for the next couple of engagements at least. We split it all down the middle, even scoring a bottle of painkillers each for that sweet, sweet full health bar.

The scene in the apartment was reminiscent of my brother's college dorm room. A bomb had very clearly gone off. Though the walls remained intact I could not say the same for the rest of the place. PBR's janky game engine and lack of destructive environments (read: indestructible buildings) did have the benefit of often keeping you safe from collateral explosive damage.

KKKatFish, or at least what was left of him, had been blown out the door and into the stairwell. His loot remained in the room and we proceeded to rifle through the rest of it after healing up.

"You want the extended mag?" Goemon asked.

"You don't want it?" I said.

"The Kar is my main, seems like a waste to put it on the AK. Until we find another one at least."

"Yeah sure, I'll take it."

Even though the Mini was semi-automatic I had a knack for dumping the ammo faster than my last girlfriend dumped me. That's unfair, though, because to tell the truth Samantha and me never actually made it that far in the first place. I just needed to ask her out first. If only I had the same confidence IRL as I did in game.

The player's loot box contained a healthy stash of ammo. The 556 went to me and the 775 went to Goemon. He could use the bigger bullet type in both of his guns which was convenient. No shotgun rounds to be had, but that was fine, I didn't need many. I pocketed enough boxes of bullets that I could be liberal with the trigger, especially now that I had an extended mag to roll with, too.

To top it all off, I found a nice cheek pad which fit over the butt of the Mini. I'm not sure exactly what it did but I did know that I needed it, bad. I aimed out the window, just to try it out. It was much more comfortable than the wood grain. Maybe it would give me the edge I needed to hit the accurate shots, maybe it would reduce recoil so I could enter rapid fire assault mode, maybe it would just make it a bit more comfortable.

The important thing was the upgraded stock put the rifle close to fully kitted. In fact, it would have been if I insisted on taking the Flash Hider. Goemon deserved it for the AK, though, he had to put something on there. It slipped over the barrel, destined to help a little bit with reigning in the bucking bronco recoil of the machine gun. Whether the weapon mod actually made a difference in hiding muzzle flash was unclear. There was never enough of a controlled environment to test out the claim.

Being fully healed and fully loaded felt incredible, but the break could not last. The cat and mouse game of the last engagement chewed up so much time off the clock that the Blue Wall of Death had initiated its hungry march across the map. To top it off, the Safety Circle was far again. It really seemed like the first placement dictated the rest of the match. If the Circle started far it would only get further. That trend continued here.

"Ah man, I don't want to run all the way down there," I groaned.

"It's not even that far," Goemon replied.

"If we run, by the time we get there it will just have moved again."

"So? We will make it without getting hurt. Then we just run to the new Circle."

"I hate the chase game."

"You want to get a car, is what you're saying."

"Oh baby. Great idea," I said.

"It was yours."

"You said it. And I think we should find The Drop, we've got time with a car. And I agree, and if it goes wrong, it's your fault and I want you to remember that."

"Alright, whatever you say, let's just check the other guy's stash first."

Big City had to contain one car, or at the very least a motorcycle. Motorcycles were so much worse because the physics of the game made it a near guarantee that getting up to speed would result in hitting a molehill, getting launched off the bike, and flying into a tree at some ungodly and nonconvertible speed in kilometers per hour. But boy, were they fun, whether they had a sidecar attached or not. There were many cars in the game, some slow, some fast, some armored, all effective so long as they had an engine and gas, and all a bit on the safer side.

As we exited the building and went around back, the bad news came first. It arrived in the form of a missing loot box. There was no sign of the body of BassMan, the other member of the conquered duo, and nothing to grab as a result. With the Blue encroaching, there was no more time to spend searching for the crate. What a waste it was to take down another enemy and not reap the benefits- just like that spring break I spent annotating Anna Karina only to find out the assignment got canceled via email the day after class got out.

Whether it was limitations of the game engine or accuracy in geographical architecture, eventually the buildings in PBR repeated themselves. Certain types got cloned a bit more often than others. For instance, the same guard tower showed up around the map. Items varied inside, but the layout and look always stayed identical.

The more pertinent example was the garage. Two types of them existed in Big City. One was what I imagined to be a Soviet 7-11, with a couple of sparse aisles inside of an efficient space. There was never anything good in them, usually just some shotgun shells or something behind the counter. It featured a corrugated metal roll-up door as an entrance, just like the second version of the building. A garage or auto mechanic's shop hid behind the door of version 2.0. Often, but not always, a car would be parked there.

"One more time, where did you last see him?" Goemon asked.

"Right around this corner. He's gone, man. Gone."

"Dang."

"It's ok, because I think I see our ticket to happiness behind door number one here."

The door shook and screeched as I pulled the chain to roll it up. The sound did not bother me, now that I knew we were the last duo standing in Big City's radius. The only thing that bothered me was the shade of grandma beige adorning the car inside the garage.

"Hey a Dosha, look at that," Goemon said.

"Wish it was the red one. I would have settled for grey sky blue," I said.

"Well now you get to settle for white. You want me to drive?"

"I think you know the answer."

"Probably a good call."

Goemon might have done most of the driving IRL- he owned the wheels, even if they were attached to the family minivan- but I handled hauling duties in game. Somehow, when he got behind the steering wheel all of his caution and patience went out the window. Often literally, as we were frequently ejected out any of the six windows of the vehicle depending on what cliff he drove off of or what tree we rammed into.

I hopped into the driver seat while my teammate got comfortable on the passenger's side. He switched to the AK and rested the barrel outside the window.

"If you were cool you'd just use the Kar for a drive by," I said.

"Stop it. Let's do this," Goemon replied.

The clown car horn sounded at the insistence of my fist. Honking that funny little horn was half the fun of driving the car, even if it always ruined the stealth approach. The build quality of the Dosha matched the duckling honk, from the miniscule ultra-subcompact frame to the one and a half cylinder engine under the hood. Still, it got great gas mileage even with four doors, and at a half a tank we could drive all over First Island. Maybe we would, so long as we avoided any big hills. Any of those would require Goemon to get out and push.

I backed the car out of the garage at full throttle and rammed into the apartment building across the alley. No serious damage, just a very small, maybe five percent hit to our health. Goemon hassled me but without good reason. It was impossible to navigate those tiny alleyways with the behemoth Dosha. Besides, we were fine and out on the open road.

The outer limits of Big City contained few notable landmarks or places worth stopping. Terrain consisted of mostly rolling grassy hills, some steep off road inclines that needed to be avoided in the Dosha, and swathes of boulders and trees just off the main path. The webbed network of roads, both paved and otherwise, connected just a few minutes' drive to the south in the same direction as the Safety Circle. The Dosha handled the gentle curves of the road just fine. After all, I was at the helm.

"You hear that?" Goemon asked.

"Oh yeah. That's the sound of the Dosha, buddy. This engine purrs like an angry lawnmower," I said.

"Man, my sound is all messed up."

"Your sound is always messed up."

"I know, I know."

"I swear I hear something. Something not the Dosha."

"Actually, I think I hear it too."

Even with my steady, expert driving skills, the trip was not a pleasure cruise. It did not take long for the sound of another vehicle to come bouncing off the hills towards us. It was likely another duo fleeing the Blue on their way to the Circle just like we were. There was still plenty of room to plot a safe course away from them. But where was the fun in that? I jerked the wheel of the Dosha, banking towards the sound of the rival motor. The game was on.

"What are you doing?" Goemon shouted from halfway out the window. My maneuver almost knocked him out of the Dosha altogether.

"We're gonna go get 'em," I replied.

It's possible the purr of the Dosha was inaudible next to the roar of the all-terrain SUV the other duo piloted. They did not appear to take any sort of evasive action as we crested a low hill, moving close enough to put the rugged Land Rover-knock-off in shooting rage. We cruised down the other side of the hill, where we lost a bit of an opportunity at a broadside by opting to dodge a boulder instead. Goemon fired a fully automatic burst anyways.

It sounded like bullets on metal to me. The SUV swerved wildly away from us and off the road as if they had just become aware of our position. If we had any sort of surprise advantage, it was gone now. We still had the more nimble Dosha which was something, but the Land Rover had armor. A straight shootout spelled disaster if the other guy had a halfway decent rifle. At this point, he probably did.

"Sounded like you hit him," I said.

"I did, like 10- how many times do you have to hit somebody in this-"

"Did you hit them or just the car?"

"I hit everything!"

Both cars were deadlocked in a parallel off road drag race until a stalwart tree forced dual swerves. The SUV fired back at us- maybe an M4 from the sound of it- but the wild steering from both drivers sent the bullets everywhere else. It was better off that way. We never shined in a broadside battle.

Instead, I eased off the gas for a moment before punching it. It was time to play tailgater. All I needed to do was follow the SUV's moves, keep a distance, and Goemon and his AK could handle the rest.

12

Drive By

The road was several kilometers back by now, which by my estimation was at least the length of multiple football fields. The terrain had flattened out and shifted from rolling rocky hills to vast pastures of wheat or hay. It had been cut recently, so visibility sat at one hundred percent. Rolled up bales the size of sideways concrete freeway supports remained as the only obstructions in the farmland.

"Think the Dosha could win against one of those?" I wondered aloud, pointing as we passed a giant wheat burrito.

"Uh, no. It's a miracle we've never hit one before."

It was no miracle. The flat field gave me more room to maneuver than a fighter pilot in outer space. The biggest threat out there sped just in front of us, and it came on four wheels. Twice the passenger stuck his body out the window, peppering bullets at us. The SUV drove so erratically that we sustained only minimal damage to the hood of the Dosha and so far no flesh wounds.

"Think you can put the wheels out in this game?" I asked.

"What, like shoot 'em?" Goemon replied.

"Yeah, does that work?"

"Of course. Remember the bridge that one time?"

Oh yeah, the bridge. I had almost forgotten about that

and why we both now had a completely rational fear of driving over bodies of water. The details of how it happened were inconsequential, but the end result did matter. It was that one time sparks flew off the right rims of our SUV as they ground across the asphalt. The vehicle caught fire briefly, but went out when it careened off the bridge and into the rocky ocean below. Needless to say, we died.

"Thanks for bringing that up. I do remember."

"The point is it's possible to shoot them. But I don't want to die," Goemon said. We swerved around another hay bale. On the return to the straightaway, I punched the throttle. It was time to close the gap.

"You'll be alright," I said.

"Oh, ok."

Another volley of gunfire sprayed us from the passenger ahead. At this distance he was able to do some actual damage. About a half dozen holes appeared in the hood of the Dosha. The windshield took it even worse as it shattered into more jagged pieces than the bottom of a Doritos bag. The glass was just as dangerous.

It looked like Goemon might have taken a bodyshot, but my focus remained on the road. He leaned out the window, which was a good sign he was healthy enough to be undeterred. As he aimed, the SUV banked right and I followed. The enemy passenger fell back into his seat. I could still see his silhouette through the back window. It showed signs of a reload in progress.

"He's reloading!" I yelled.

"I see that," Goemon shouted back from outside the window. He fired off maybe a third of a clip. "Try and keep it steady."

"I mean I'm trying," I said. "This guy's nuts."

As I tried to maintain distance with the enemy duo, I

looked ahead for orientation. We were rapidly running out of field to cover. The hit job would have to finish soon, before the chance disappeared for good.

Goemon stretched out the window again for another attempt. The Dosha held steady for long enough to offer him a clean shot. He took advantage, unloading the rest of the mag and blowing out the back right tire. A chunk of rubber flew in through the absent windshield. The SUV sunk towards the ground and lost a touch of speed but other than that plowed onward, unaffected.

I expected something between an instant explosion and a cartwheel of scrap metal, but it looked as though we mostly just caused an inconvenience and the enemy duo would be fully reloaded by now. Maybe if Goemon ended up with that extended mag he could have taken out two tires. Oh well.

A steep and roadless mountain lingered beyond the edge of the field. It was just a few seconds away. Even with the bum wheel, the engine of the SUV would carry it right up and over. The Dosha, damaged and puny, could never climb the slope.

"Let's bail. He's about to blow us away," Goemon said as the other player prepared to fire.

"Time for the driver to drive," I said.

"What-"

I squeezed out whatever juice remained in the lemon that was the Dosha and caught up to the SUV. I swerved right, preparing to execute the classic pit maneuver. Goemon fell back inside, both of us taking a shot or two to the vest. I ignored it. With any luck, a solid hit to the corner of the other vehicle would cause it to flip as a result of the blown tire.

"Hold on tight!" I called out. Of course, there was nothing for him to hold except for the AK and that would not help him anymore. The Dosha, still parallel to the SUV, closed the gap, leaving about a yard- or a meter I guess- of space between the two vehicles. The field disappeared behind us, the mountain maybe a second in front.

I jerked the wheel to the left, but the car failed to respond. Everything slowed down, which made it slightly easier to figure out what went wrong. I looked out the driver side window. Then, down. Ah, there was the problem. At least two wheels of the Dosha appeared to be off the ground. The side view mirror confirmed the suspicion. The whole car was airborne, thanks to a strategically placed bump in the road. The SUV sped off up the hill, leaving a cloud of dust behind.

They were the least of our worries now, and it was probably in our favor that the enemy duo did not rip the e-brake, hop out of the car and light us up right there. We would probably never see them again. We were probably about to die.

"Oh no," Goemon said calmly.

No. It was not over. The driver had to drive. I cranked the wheels the other direction, fully prepared to correct the fishtail when the Dosha hit the ground. It smashed into the dirt, and it did not spin out, which was great. But, the momentum and the questionable physics of jumping vehicles in the game was enough to be a death sentence for the car. The little vehicle bounced, sideways, and flipped three or four times. It stopped eventually and the world was upside down.

The passenger seat lay empty. Goemon's voice slipped in my ears between all of the ringing bells. All I knew was he was somewhere else, and he was alive. Fortunately, the Dosha boasted safety regulations requiring a whopping total of zero seat belts so that left nothing that needed to be cut to release me from my inverted aluminum prison. Good thing, too, because all I had for a knife was a frying pan, and that sounded like an awful game mechanic anyways.

"What the heck man," Goemon shouted from the north, behind me. His voice was becoming more clear. I stumbled out the window of the Dosha and checked myself for any major leaks. Everything seemed fine, and health still sat at about a third full, which was better than two thirds empty.

Even though the ground tried to spiral away from me, I tested my feet to see if they worked. I stumbled a bit but managed to stay upright as I turned around and headed towards my teammate. He was downed, a short ways back towards the flat field, helpless to anyone who might be watching.

"Hurry up!" he shouted. It concerned him, clearly.

"It's OK," I replied. My voice sounded funny to my ears, even more so than normal. It was like I left the Listen function on my mic. "They drove away. We scared 'em good." Now that I said it I turned around to make sure it was true. No sign of the SUV, at least. Perhaps they parked it on the other side of the mountain with the idea of finishing the job on foot. Probably not. They wanted to get out of there. We did scare them. Even if they did intend to come back, it meant we had some time. No way they could land accurate shots from that far based on their prior shooting.

I reached Goemon in the clearing. He was crawling towards an enormous bale of hay, instinctively trying to hide from the other duo. Always better to be safe. He seemed a bit upset, but I had yet to figure out why. I figured the best thing for me to do was lighten the mood a little bit. I pulled out a first aid kit and started to heal myself.

"You've gotta be kidding me. Pick me up!" Goemon shouted.

"What good are we if we don't have any health?" I asked, straight faced.

"Oh my- I'm going to die, jerk."

I put the first aid kit away. "It was just a joke! I was just joshing around. You know, a goof." I began picking him up. That made one knock for each of us.

"Where are they?" Goemon asked.

"Long gone."

"That's good, I guess." He stood up and brushed himself off before we both started first aid. "What exactly happened?"

"I hit a bump, I guess."

"A bump."

"Well it doesn't take much, you know that."

"It's a miracle we're still alive at all."

"That's the spirit. This is the Round of Destiny."

"Don't say that."

"I think it's true."

"You'll jinx it."

"We've been getting pretty lucky so far. I think it can continue," I said. Somebody had to be optimistic around here. Sometimes, a round of PBR came down to just flat out luck. Actually, they more often came down to being unlucky. You find a gun or you don't, you find a car or you don't. Helmet, armor, you end up outside the Circle or in it. Forget being lucky. The absence of unluckiness was enough to get the W.

As soon as I finished my sentiment, the Dosha exploded. I fell backwards from the shock. Good thing we got out of there. The combination of the battle damage and its inverted state must have pushed it over the edge.

"I'm going to miss that ol' girl," I said longingly.

"No you won't. That thing was a piece," Goemon laughed.

"How dare you."

"What's the plan now?"

"Aside from revenge?"

"Revenge is probably good enough."

The car chase was not a complete exercise in futility. We did not get our kill, and we lost our car. Also, Goemon broke a hip. But we did make it several kilometers in the right direction. The Blue would not threaten us for the immediate future at least.

"Maybe they'll be on the other side of that hill, in that town," Goemon said.

"I mean we got nothing better to do. Besides, we will have the advantage on the hilltop."

It was a rare round in which both of us had a sniper rifle. I wanted to put them to use, even if I was a terrible shot at a distance. Those guys in the SUV kind of sucked anyways. If they were better than halfway decent we would be dead.

We began the arduous climb up the hill. It did not require ropes and hooks or anything, but the incline prevented us from using full foot speed. A plateau at the top of the hill obscured our vision of the top. It was possible that the enemy duo could be sitting up there waiting for us, but I think I knew them well enough at this point to say they were scared babies who would be taking refuge in the town at the bottom of the hill. I knew their type, too terrified to engage in a real duel like a gentleman. Always on the run, hoping to let everyone else kill each other until it came down to the end. Just in case my instincts were wrong, which was never, we moved from tree to tree as we trekked up the hill, using the trunks as cover.

"You hear that?" I asked.

"No."

"Listen."

"Is that the SUV?"

"That's what I'm saying."

But the roar was too loud at the distance it came from to be a car. This was a different vehicle, one that we could not drive but could get just as much benefit from. This was The Drop plane, and it was headed in our direction. How not unlucky.

"Hey, when one door closes, another opens," I said.

13

The Drop

Ah, The Drop. The forbidden fruit. Just like the classic story in the Bible where the snake offers Eve a mystery box with an M249 heavy machine gun and she takes it but the snake's magical monkey paw curls a finger and her duo partner Adam gets gunned down as a result. Only this was no fairy tale.

This was real life. Technically it was virtual life but this was just as important and way better anyways. The stakes remained the same. The Drop represented the highest risk and the highest reward. The crate itself contained (hopefully) the best weapons in the round, but sometimes the cost of admission was early termination.

A cargo plane, not unlike the one all the competitors rode in on at the start of the match, soared in across some pre-determined flight path. You could hear it and see it from far and wide. Only this plane carried something infinitely better than trash-talking scrubs. If you happen to be in a lucky spot when the bay doors open, then you've got a solid chance at becoming the proud owner of some serious firepower. Of course, when the plane drops the payload from five thousand feet up, the crate is attached to several deployed parachutes to ensure safe descent. It takes a couple of minutes for The Drop to touch down. While it's in the sky, anyone that hears the commotion need only look up to determine the location of the aforementioned treasure chest.

From there, it's not just a race to the landing site to stake claim. You also have to fight off whoever else has their eyes on the loot. Aside from the initial landing at the start of the round, The Drop is often one of the most heavily contested parts of the game. That also made it pretty fun.

To be fair, securing the loot from The Drop did not guarantee a win of the round. Sometimes you struck out on getting anything good, rendering all the work of getting to the thing frustrating and pointless. Most of the time, though, the weapon or weapons inside would lead to a significant advantage for the rest of the game. It was less of an autoaim hack and more the equivalent of the Super Mario fire flower.

"We gotta go get it," I said.

"Hm," Goemon replied. It always took a bit of coaxing. The Drop had led to our demise probably more times than it had done otherwise. But the loot! The adventure!

"Come on. Come on. Come onnn."

"We can at least scope it out."

"Alright! That's what I'm talking about."

"At the top of the hill."

"Of course!"

"And if it looks sketchy we bail out."

"That seems perfectly reasonable."

"I mean it, I'm not getting killed over some loot dream."

"Hey, me neither. Let's get up there then."

We abandoned the strategy of sneaking from tree to tree. If anyone had been waiting to ambush us at the top of the slope, they would have seen The Drop, too. If anyone saw The Drop from that close, they would have been unable to resist the chance to be first to make contact.

Boulders and trees dotted the plateau at the top of the

hill. They would do nicely to provide cover from either side of the embankment. Elevation should be an advantage. However, utilizing it often came down to whether we could actually land our shots at a distance.

We both crouched low upon approaching the opposite crest of the plateau. From there, we got a clear view of the small "town" at the foot of the hill. It was about the size of The Spot- just a few houses, only one of them two stories. An asphalt road ran through the town and off to who knows where. The SUV sat parked in the middle of it. The SUV Duo made no effort to hide the vehicle, or their intentions. Couple of amateurs, those guys.

Just off the base of the hill on the street, a set of four deflated parachutes laid sprawled out in the clearing. In the center of them stood a Dosha-size wooden shipping crate. The rest of the area looked empty.

"Why haven't they gotten it yet?" I asked.

"I don't know. They left their car running, right there," Goemon replied.

"Weird. Maybe they're waiting to see who else goes after it."

"That's what we're doing."

"Ah, man, you don't want to go get it? It's right there."

"Not yet."

"Alright, alright."

"We have sniper rifles, remember. We should probably use them."

The allure of The Drop was hard to resist, especially at that distance. But I had to resist or pay the price. Someone else needed to test the waters first. You do not want to embarrass yourself as the first person on the dance floor, after all.

I peered through the scope for a closer look. An 8x magnification would have been great in that situation, but the 3x scope proved markedly better than the naked eye. Goemon joined in with his own rifle, though he laid flat on the ground for maximum stability and stealth.

"Left side," Goemon said.

I shifted the sight to the left of the crate and saw a helmet with a full face mask. It was a level three, freshly pulled out of The Drop by one of the guys from the SUV duo. Then, as soon as the helmet had popped into view, it disappeared back behind the crate. They were using The Drop itself for cover against us—or they just got lucky and ended up on the proper side.

"They're both behind there, I think," he continued.

"Sonofa- they're getting the loot."

"They are."

"You shoot 'em, you can take him out."

"Not with that helmet."

"Well you shoot him first and I'll finish 'em off."

"What about the other guy?"

"Can't worry about that now."

"OK, sure."

"I wonder what gun they got."

"Hopefully nothing good."

"No, hopefully it was super good and we can kill them and take it and then we'll have something super good."

"Yeah unless they kill us first."

"Dangit man, we can't worry about that now!"

"I think someone else is coming."

A high-pitched whir bounced off the hills, rapidly gaining volume. Instinct removed my finger from its place on the trigger. Goemon's wait-and-see strategy became the priority. The player with the level three helmet heard the engine, too.

He spun around in a circle, even looking in our general direction, but not long enough to spot us. He could not pin down the source, probably due to echo.

They would solve the mystery in a moment as a motorcycle roared into view from around the hill. It was a second duo, come for The Drop. This made three total duos including ourselves, all forming a triangle with the sought-after prize in the center. Our location atop the mountain placed us somewhere between the other two. The middle of a firefight was not the place to be, but we were far enough back to stay out of view. Besides, we had the crucial tactical advantage of being undetected.

"Another duo," Goemon said.

We had no reason to shoot at that point. It was better to let the rest of them duke it out. We could mop up the survivors afterwards. At least that was what conventional wisdom would have you believe. But I'm pretty sure if Sun Tzu got to choose between playing god and deciding who lived and who died or just playing it safe he would take the former. This was the Coliseum and I was the Roman emperor! Thumbs up! Thumbs down!

"Now, to sit down and watch the truth of battle or decide the victor myself with a well-placed shot from the Mini, gimping a duo, leaving them ripe for the picking as-"

"Whoa man," Goemon said.

"Oh. Right. Sorry. Who you got?" I asked.

"Hm. Well, let's see here."

The motorcycle, a street model with an attached sidecar, screeched to a halt behind a boulder big enough to provide cover. The two players hopped out and crouched, out of the line of fire. They had a sort of calm togetherness about them, displayed by a lack of movements. Park bike, get out, hide, no hesitation, no excess. The outfits did not hurt, either. Underneath the armor-level two helmets and vests by the look of it-the duo sported identical tracksuits, primarily gold with purple stripes running down the side. It was not camo, but man it looked professional. Maybe Goemon and I needed to invest some credits into matching gear.

Meanwhile, the SUV Duo rolled around to the outside of the crate. They did not exude serenity, instead poking their heads up and around the cover of their crate. They had the weapons to get the job done, though.

"Looks like the bikers got a couple ARs. M4, kitted. Nice. I don't even know what the other one is," Goemon said.

I took the opportunity to scope in on the SUV Duo. "Well, the other guys have one level three helmet for sure and maybe a couple level three vests. And...oh boy."

"What?" Goemon asked.

"Looks like there was a Para in the Drop."

The rapid pops of gunfire commenced. The initial volley came from Biker Duo behind the rock, probably trying to take advantage of the other team peeking out all over the place.

"Oh man, if there's a Para involved, I don't know," Goemon said.

"Yeah but will they be able to use it?" I asked. The M249 Para was my personal best case scenario as a Drop weapon, or really just a PBR weapon at all. It could shoot something like a hundred bullets before needing a reload, and had manageable recoil on top of that. It was the very definition of spray and pray, so long as you had the ammunition- or remembered to load it. I watched the Para guy lean out and shoot with a click. He ducked back down and scrambled to load it.

"This guy just peeked and forgot to load it. He's not even the one with the helmet," I said.

"Oh no."

"Come on, let's just take these guys down! Just one shot!"

I pleaded.

"What, so both duos can turn and light us up?"

"No, I guess not."

"Biker duo is about to throw a nade."

A well-placed nade was a thing of beauty. Like sinking a three-pointer from downtown in basketball, but with the elegance of chipping in a shot for a birdie in golf. Of course, I had never played either sport but the concept was the same. I ditched the scope for the moment to get the bird's eye view, just in time to see the motorcycle guy hurl the grenade. It arced high and bounced off the top of the Drop crate, hitting with the exact amount of force it needed to rebound right between the well-armored SUV Duo. The toss was a textbook example of a grenade hurl, a mastery of physics.

The timing could have used some work though. The canister rolled on the ground for a second or two, enough time for the two teammates to evacuate in opposite directions. The Biker Duo opened fire.

I peered into the scope again for a closer look. It was a terrible decision. As the SUV Duo fled, the grenade exploded in a blinding white flash. Turns out it was a grenade of the stun variety, not the explosive kind. To be fair they both probably would have blinded me for staring right at them but now I was fairly certain I would never see again.

I yelped, and Goemon laughed. "Oh wow, look at what they're doing here," he said.

"I'm blind. Permanently!" I yelled. I heard the echoes of gunfire all around, but I saw nothing but white.

"This is great stuff. The tactics, man. The counter attack."

"What? What's happening?"

"Well, Biker Duo threw a stun nade, just a great nade. I

guess you saw that."

"Yeah, jerk."

"Oh! Oh man, I can't believe he pulled that off."

"What? What?"

"Ok so the nade goes down and the Drop Duo scatter, but they're for sure blind."

"Are they still alive?" I asked, but the drumroll of machine gun fire gave me my answer. I could discern maybe just two now, maybe only one firing with an echo.

"So the one with the Para, he just starts unloading a thousand bullets. I don't even know if he can see 'em."

"And? And?"

"And then he- hang on, I have to land this shot."

14

Head's Up

The whip crack of the Kar sniper rifle next to me did a number on my ears. It was loud enough to distract me from my temporary blindness. I may have been a little premature with my declaration of permanence on that front. The shapes of the world were starting to take form. A tree branch here, a boulder there. But The Drop and the dueling duos were gone. Oh, wait, I was just facing the wrong direction. Must have turned around while blinded.

Another bolt of lightning set off a cannonball next to my ear, oh, actually that was just Goemon shooting his rifle again. By that point I could see well enough to join the fray. The only problem being I was clueless as to which players were still kicking down there.

"Where?" I asked, raising the Mini through the white haze of my vision.

"Behind the rock. He's so lit. I shot him but then I missed," Goemon replied.

This was the moment I had been training my whole life for. Or at the very least the several months that we had been playing the game. I held my breath and found nothing to shoot but the backside of a boulder. He must have ducked behind it. I sighed out all the air at once, like a deflated balloon. Great.

"I take it he knows we're here now."

"Oh he knows we're here. But he's the last one left."

"OK, so we just wait for him to peek and-"

Goemon fired again. In the upper right corner of the HUD, his name appeared next to the words Kar98 and Groovy-Chronic. Guess he got him. Don't get me wrong, part of me was happy but man I wanted some action and that was my shot, literally. Ah, who am I kidding, my teammate deserved it. I had to look at the stupid flash.

"OK actually now he's the last one left," Goemon said as he pulled back the lever on the Kar.

"Are you sure?" I asked. Maybe I might just get my shot after all.

"Yeah, yeah, that was just his knocked buddy. I shot him in the toe, it was all I could see."

"Ouch. Poor guy."

"He was super hurt."

A cloud of dust kicked up in front of us, and Goemon rolled behind the safety of his nearby rock. I would do no such thing. With the other player focused on Goemon's location I had at least a second before the bullets got trained on me. I peered through the scope, happy to have a stationary target, and I forgot to hold my breath this time. I pulled the trigger and it did not matter. A message flashed across the middle of my screen with confirmation the shot was as accurate as it needed to be. I looked up at the action center of the HUD, just to see my name up there. There it was, Field with a headshot from the- what! How was that not a headshot? That is some BS right there. But, at least I got the kill, and it felt real good.

"I got him!" I yelled out.

"Dude nice," Goemon said.

"That was all of them?"

"Yeah man. Biker Duo took out one of them that got flashed immediately. But the guy with the Para went crazy, he lit them up. It might have been an accident, I'm pretty sure he was blind."

Now that the shot had been fired and the engagement was over, the adrenaline subsided. My vision and hearing returned to normal. I realized that my pulse was firing faster than that light machine gun. The whole experience made me feel a bit numb and the end of the round was still far off.

I got up out of cover and sprinted for the loot of The Drop and all the fallen players around it. Goemon told me to wait, but there was no time for that. The loot, the loot!

Every once in a while, some aspect of PBR works out so flawlessly, so perfect, that it makes you feel like you have destiny on your side. I'm talking about The fabled Round of Destiny. Of course, I knew better. Take that encounter, for instance- no luck there. We made our own destiny. The reason we still stood to fight another duo was purely our skill in the game, our tactical knowledge, our intense scrutiny and memorization of all quadrants of the map, and general mastery of game mechanics.

"Are we the greatest PBR players of all time?" I pondered.

"No," Goemon responded.

It was just like Goemon to try and bring us back down to Earth. I could see his point, eventually, while I was free falling into the cavern. I forgot about the "entrance" to that cavern. A big hole in the side of a mountain, about the size of a swimming pool. The edge was mostly covered by low shrubbery, but you could still see the opening if you were looking for it. I was not looking for it.

The Cave, we called it. We used to like to drop there, but the towns around it never had anything good so it never seemed worth it. Now it was time to relive our glory days, I guess. I opened up the map to see if there was a glitch that removed it from my screen. Nope, the entrance was there, unmarked with text but nonetheless designated by a dark blue kidney bean.

Maybe I slipped in my excitement to get to the Para. Maybe the game glitched out- it was not uncommon, after all- and teleported me into the opening of the cave. Maybe it was just lag and I rubber banded in there. Probably I was just an idiot.

The time spent in midair plummet probably only consisted of a second or two. It was enough time to come to the conclusion that I messed up.

Fortunately, The Cave was designed to be explored. The underground lake within existed solely to prevent death from falling. You could still die if you hit the shore, but my angle looked good. I hit the water and floated back to the surface, still alive, but now several stories underground.

The sky, grey as it was, blinded through the gap compared to the darkness of the rest of the cavern. The hole in the ceiling of the cave and floor of the mountain seared its bean visage into my retina. A silhouette stood out on the edge. It was Goemon, no doubt, peering over the side.

"Get down here! Hurry! I don't want to die alone," I yelled up to him.

"What are you doing down there?" he hollered back.

"I fell."

My eyes readjusted. Goemon looked from side to side, then hopped into the hole. For whatever reason, he usually ended up being the one to hit the rocks of the underground shore. The jump's trajectory looked sketchy at first but he splashed into the water nonetheless. I swam the couple of meters to the stone shore and figured I would make the best of the situation by looting.

"What was that you were saying? Before you fell in here?" Goemon asked. I can only assume he was being facetious.

"I was saying that I planned on dropping down here because I wanted us both to have freshly tailored level 2 vests. Now come grab one of these."

Bland grey stone comprised the majority of The Cave. The rest was wood scaffolding and some columns in disrepair. I think it was originally intended to be some sort of archaeological dig site, but the full textures of the place made it look unfinished by the devs. Of course, they would probably come up with some explanation about how IRL work on it had been finished but it was intended to look unfinished in game because the excavators never got a chance to complete it.

Sometimes there was decent loot down there. But unless you were first to reach it and got lucky with something really good, it put you at a disadvantage strategically. It seems absurd to think that someone would actually shoot fish in a barrel but the very concept applied here. To top it off, there wasn't exactly a fifty foot wooden ladder stretching out the crack in the mountain. That left only two ways out of the place, a deathtrap of a long tunnel out one side and a waterway out to the river that worked just fine so long as a jet ski happened to spawn in the underground lake.

"You really do care," I said to Goemon. To think, after all that work upstairs, he would throw it all away to make sure I was ok.

"Something like that. You know, I don't think we were alone up there."

"We weren't. We took those duos down."

"That's not what I mean."

I climbed the scaffolding, looking for a better helmet or something better for the Mini. "You got to be kidding me."

"I think I hear somebody."

"How, we're inside of a mountain. Covered in stone."

"I don't know, the sound doesn't make any sense in this game."

I stopped moving and listened hard. The faint echo of footsteps bounced around the roughly dome-shaped interior of The Cave. They got a bit louder and appeared to emanate from The Drop, but it was hard to tell. The sound in PBR was wonky indeed, and directional audio interpretation really broke down when different heights got involved.

Goemon and I each found a different stone column to duck behind. We looked towards the gateway to the sky.

"Hey idiots," a nasally voice called down. The voice carried a bunch of background noise with it. He either had a terrible mic or a lot going on at his house.

"Ha HA," the other one said, a bit more clear. The laugh was fake, Muntzian. I had yet to zero in on their silhouettes peering down on us. Perhaps they had yet to lean over.

"You see them?" I whispered to Goemon.

"No. Above us, somewhere," he replied.

"Wow, you guys are so bad. Holy crap you guys are bad. It's like what are you even doing playing this game," the one said out of his nostrils.

"Yeah, get good," his partner said.

"More like get a life," the nose snorted.

"Ha HA, good one."

They did not see us. Otherwise, they would have opened fire. Goemon tried to shush me but I could no longer resist. "Well which one is it? Get good or get a life."

"Get- uh, shut up nerd," the nose said. He must have been the leader, but it did not take much to overload his brain. "Thanks for clearing out The Drop for us. Even if you didn't fall down there we would have killed you anyways just so you know."

"Just so you know, we jumped down here on purpose," I continued. I never was much for trash talking. Usually by the time I produced a decent rebuttal the moment was long over.

"No, you fell. Otherwise you would have got the loot. Which we got, by the way, level 3 vests and everything. We're so good now."

I could not believe they equipped the level three vests. Those things would be shredded after that firefight, probably worse than a fresh level one. These guys were the worst, and we were going to take them down. Goemon got the same idea, nodding his head and pointing to the south corner of the entrance. He readied the Kar98, careful to keep it hidden from view. I did the same with my rifle.

"We left it on purpose," I said. Man that was bad. But these guys were stupid. I had to figure out another story. "Left it...because...there was something way better down here."

"What?"

"Yeah, you probably never even heard of it. Just got patched into the game."

"Let me see," the kid wheezed. The silhouette emerged, and Goemon and I both fired. He went down immediately, but unfortunately remained above the fold. I could hardly believe the guy took the bait, but we only got one of them. He crawled back out of view as the other began raining bullets down upon us.

Dirt and stone dust swirled around the onslaught. As long as we stayed behind the columns we could stay alive. The Para was really the perfect weapon to shoot into The Cave, or outside of it, or into a building, or out of a car, or really anywhere. So close to being mine. Always, so, so close, like landing a kickflip for the first time except you just shatter your ankle bones instead.

"What the (inaudible), Jeffie! Get back here and pick me

the (inaudible) up!" the guy yelled. Someone in the background of his microphone chimed in, a feminine voice that sounded angry. She said something about using language under her roof.

"I'm going to get them," the one now referred to as Jeffie said.

"No, they're my kill, I'm going to die, pick me up. Me!" said the first. It was tough to tell but he might have been fighting back tears.

"OK," Jeffie said sadly. He must have had no choice. The hail of bullets stopped.

15

Boat Rental

"We need to bail. We won't get another shot like that," Goemon said.

"But we rekt that guy," I said.

"True." He left his post, still crouched, and hustled toward the tunnel at the mouth of the sunken lake.

"True, but..."

"But they know we're here now so if we peek we'll get destroyed."

"Fair enough."

"Jet ski?" he asked.

"Jet ski!" I of course replied.

This time, Goemon took the reins. It was not so much because he did not trust my driving anymore. We all had accidents, right? Like just because that one time in the Taco Bell drive-thru he plowed into the speaker box I wasn't just going to stop getting in the van if he was driving. No, this time Goemon got to drive because he got to the jet ski first and that is just how the PBR game engine worked. You could switch from driver to passenger in an SUV or Dosha but spots were set on watercraft for some unknown game logic reason.

By the time we climbed aboard the two-man boat, really

more of the equivalent of a water motorcycle, the enemy duo above had opened up the floodgates of destruction again. The machine gun fire tore up our old hiding place first. It only took a second after that for them to spot us. A wake of bullets trailed behind us all the way to the tunnel, but they never quite figured out how to compensate for speed. If they did, they would have aimed ahead. Once we hit the exit tunnel there was nothing the other duo could do.

The tunnel was a short passage out of the sunken cave. It only took a few seconds' travel by jet ski. Swimming manually rendered the route unusable, though. You swam about as fast as the cool kids walked the mile in protest during freshman year gym class. If you had to swim at all, you might as well drown before the Blue or the bullets got you.

"Why is this thing made out of wood?" I asked.

"No idea. Because wood floats?"

"I guess so."

"What would you make it out of?"

As we rounded the bend of the underpass, the sun basked us in its unassuming hazy glow. Freedom, and once again I felt good. Even if I still feel like we could have taken them.

"I don't know, plastic or fiberglass or something, isn't that what they're made out of?"

"I dunno. East or west?"

"Huh?"

"Left or right."

"Uh." I pulled out the map. I might have known the roads like the back of my hand. Sometimes. But water navigation required reference. "If we go right we'll probably get our hair cut by the Para."

"Left, then," Goemon said.

"Cool. Just beach it over by that hill and we can go to the radio tower."

"The radio tower never has anything good."

"Ah, but if you already have a sniper rifle it's not so bad. We should have enough time before the Blue rolls in."

"I guess. The super scopes are hard to use."

"It'll be fun. Come on, remember that one time we won the round a long time ago because you had the 8x scope and you shot all the way across two towns to take down the last guy?"

"No."

"Well, it was cool. Let's do it again."

I do not remember if the round in question played out exactly like that. It's possible I got the circumstances switched and we were actually the ones who got sniped from three miles or eight kilometers away and I only have the kill cam footage seared into my memory. Goemon was good enough to do it. He just needed to believe in himself. Besides, a bigger scope for my own rifle would be just the thing to kick the round into high gear.

The radio tower possessed the allure of being the highest place on First Island. It was tucked smack dab in the middle of what qualified as the mountainous region. Only an SUV with a running start could make it up that slope, and few had the willpower to endure the trek on foot. Perhaps because it was the uppermost point, the frequency of sniper rifle mods spawning up there was quite high. It was one example of the occasional attention to detail present in the game.

The hike to the top was mostly uneventful. The great wall of the Blue became the most prominent feature of the 360-degree view, a digital ocean on a tsunami timer poised to submerge all but two players or in many cases even one. The entire world (map) flooded in biblical fashion, and you could survive if you built your ark out of enough bullets and the tools that shot them. Then, the round restarted and the great Blue beast slumbered again if only for the several minute warm-up period.

"Really makes you think," I said.

"About what?"

"I don't know man, you ever think there's more out there beyond the Blue WOD, past the digital ocean."

"Don't know. An invisible wall, probably."

"Yeah, probably."

"You could play offline and go noclip to try and find out."

"It's just like, we're here, fighting for our lives. We don't even stop to talk to these people."

"So."

"So? Don't you want to know the motivation? Why they're here? Why they do the grind night in and night out, the spawning, the dropping, the looting, the killing, the more looting, the inevitable dying?"

"You really want to go back and talk to those clowns at The Cave? They're all like that."

He had a point. The optional anonymity mixed with the brevity of the interactions made a lot of players come off as dumb. The excessive profanity and often overt racism and accompanying slurs did nothing to bolster the reputation of the average PBR-er. The disgruntled mom in the background did nothing to help the situation, either.

Maybe that was unfair, though. Maybe the average PBR player had more going on upstairs, and it was just a very vocal minority that made the rest of us look bad. We were not that obnoxious. OK sometimes we were, but usually it was only if provoked. Also the crazy racial slur guy only popped up like once or twice a round. The girls we met seemed OK.

"What about the girls?" I asked.

"Who?"

"You know. The girls that went to The Spot."

"Oh. What about them?"

"They didn't seem so bad."

"No, they were alright I guess."

"Maybe we should have had a little chat."

"Oh, just a nice little chat."

"Yeah!"

"They would have killed us, man. You've lost it."

"I'm just saying."

"OK, maybe next round we can try and have a conversation with somebody, but we're pretty far in here."

Yeah, they probably would have killed us if we tried to stay and chat. But sometimes I liked to think about the people on the other side of the barrier. Maybe we really could have hit it off, exchanged info. Became friends. Lovers. Ah, who am I kidding, PBR was a terrible place to meet girls.

I managed to talk our way to the top of the mountain. Goemon searched the inside while I swept the outside. Nothing too useful but I did find bullet loops for the Kar98. I think they made it easier to reload but I really did not know.

The radio tower was like everything else on First Island: mostly broken but intact enough to give you the general idea of what it represented. The metal antenna had been cracked in half, making it impossible to climb. A crumbled concrete staircase almost led to a metal catwalk, but did not quite get there. That was fine, the base of the tower was high enough already.

Besides, the view always ended up being a bit disappointing. Limitations of the PBR game engine reduced the distant visibility to a mostly hazy fog. The remote terrain and mountains arose as featureless mounds of unworked clay, with only the biggest trees able to be displayed. The only other details that showed up were different players, so long as they were running. Even they appeared as ants across a blank background, like the two I could see to the upper right. I mean, southeast.

"I see someone. Actually two," I said calmly. No need to panic, the other duo was kilometers away. We were invisible to them.

"Where?"

"South...easty. I mean, like 130. Ish."

"Those guys are so far."

"Good thing you got the Kar. Here, I got you a present." I tossed him the bullet loops modification to do whatever it did.

"Oh hey, it's fully kitted. You want this 4x scope?"

"Heck yeah. You don't want it?"

"No, I found an eight-by inside."

"Oh, baby."

"I know."

"Now you got no excuse."

"You mean except that it's impossible."

"Come on, you might as well give it a shot. We came all the way up here."

"I mean, you're right."

"I'll be the spotter," I offered.

"OK. Do I go prone? Or crouch on a knee?"

"How should I know?"

"I guess I'll lay down. This thing sways so much. It's real difficult."

"Don't worry, you got this."

I equipped Goemon's old scope on the Mini rifle and it

brought the distant world into focus. Much of the detail returned, but the players still contrasted against the background, nothing more than a flat, empty field. The duo donned level three gear. Either there was a ton of it floating around, or they were the same jokers from the cavern.

"I think they're the same guys," I noted.

"I think you're right."

"Which one you gonna go for first?"

"I don't know, the one in the front. That guy was the worst."

"How can you tell the difference?"

"I can't, really. They're both the worst."

"OK, I got him spotted."

Goemon fired the first round. A cloud of dirt erupted several meters away from the target. It was a bad first shot, but we were pretty far. This was probably a personal record attempt for distance.

"Miss, two low, and behind him," I called.

"Dang, that was too low? I aimed like a foot over his head."

"Aim higher, I guess. Your gun is from one of the World Wars or something, it can probably barely make it."

"I thought you said it would be fine!"

"It will be, come on, come on, before they hide."

Goemon cranked the bolt back, loading another round. The duo did the opposite of hide, opting instead for a shelter in place strategy. They both crouched down in a horrid interpretation of a phalanx. From there, they stumbled over each other, spinning around, trying to determine the source of the shot. I considered trying my luck at sniping them with the weaker scope but I figured Goemon could take another crack at it first.

"OK, at least they stopped running. I'm going to aim way above."

He fired again, and a beautiful shot, perfectly executed. I could practically hear the gong sound as the guy's level three helmet flew off. Unfortunately he remained upright.

"How is he not dead? This game doesn't make any sense," Goemon said.

"Guess the level three helmet really makes a difference. Even if it's damaged, apparently."

I aimed high, a full body length above the player's head. I fired and the scope kicked up so I could not even see if I landed the shot. I fired twice more, figuring I might as well take advantage of the semiautomatic nature of my weapon of choice. Maybe I should have been laying down instead because I did not know what I was shooting at. My scope stopped shaking again and by some miracle I had landed at least one of the shots, enough to knock the wounded target.

"You got him," Goemon said.

"I don't know how. I aimed like fifty feet over his head. Is his buddy really about to pick him up right now?"

"That's a terrible idea."

Rather than taking cover, the remaining member of the duo- most likely Jeffie, being screamed at by his partner- chose to kneel down, completely stationary. He had to follow orders, and orders must have been to revive, revive! The shot could not have been more lined up. Goemon took advantage and fired true. As Jeffie collapsed so did the other.

I looked at the scoreboard. Field finally killed xXx-ScOp3ShOwxXx. It was nice to get credit for the kill after a successful knock. It was even better to get revenge on those jerks. The scope worked, the rifle worked, the plan, everything actually worked out for once.

"Did that really just happen?" I asked.

"What?"

"Did we just snipe a duo? Successfully?"

"We got this, baby," Goemon said as he reloaded the Kar.

16

Salt Flats

"Do we have time to make it down there? Before the Blue rolls in?" I asked.

"I'm tired of getting kills and leaving loot," Goemon said.

I hated dying from the Blue. It was such a long, drawn out process, one that you fought and fought against until the bitter end even if you knew it was fruitless. I have to imagine it was similar to being stranded out in the middle of the ocean and trying to swim to shore. You are going to try, because you can't just give up. If you do, that's the end. But you know you will never make it. At least in the ocean you might get lucky and come up on an island, or a boat or plane, or a giant friendly humpback whale that offers to carry you all the way back to the mainland. It is something to fight for. It was way worse in PBR than in real life. Maybe not really, but seriously, it was worse. If the Safety Circle appeared at the opposite corner of the map and you got swallowed up by the hungry Blue monster you just kept running, taking damage faster and faster until you died. And you died alone, killed by no one but bad luck and your own poor planning. Sure, you could stop and heal, but while you did so the Blue just kept going, doing even more damage than it did when you stopped to bust out the first aid or the bandages. But you still thought about it. Your health ticks down, two thirds, half. There's still time to heal, you think. Wait any longer and you will be dead before the first aid finishes. So you kneel down to heal and open up your map while the first aid works its magic and the Circle is eighteen kilometers away, and you will never make it, but you try anyway and die. An embarrassing message flashes to everyone in the scoreboard, just so all the players know you did not get shot by somebody better, but you got left behind, like getting picked last for kickball everyday all over again.

Despite all of these horrible reasons, the Blue and the position of the Safety Circle failed to rank on Goemon's importance scale. In his mind, a gun and some decent cover was all you needed to get out of any situation in PBR. He played a meticulous game in every other aspect of a round. It always came down to me being the one concerned about death by environment.

I checked the clock. I scanned the map. I tried to look at it through the lens of my ally. Usually when I did that I survived way longer. We still had a few minutes left.

"We can do it. But we gotta hustle. I might even go so far as to say we have to book it," I said. To be fair, I was also tired of missing out on all the victory spoils.

"Whoa whoa, cool your jets," Goemon said.

"I just don't want to-"

"Die from the Blue."

"Yeah, let's just go already."

The jaunt down the mountain was easier than the road up. We picked up some speed on the way down but it only took one glitchy rock face before you were falling in midair for twenty feet wondering what happened.

"I just want to say, whatever happens, it's been a good round so far," I said.

"Yeah it's been alright," Goemon replied.

"No, I mean, we've done it all, right? Got to The Spot, we got some good loot. Won a few engagements. Heck we even sniped some fools."

"Yeah."

"More importantly, we had a good time doing it. Just quality time, you know? Just a couple guys, hanging out. This is what it's all about."

"You OK, man?"

"Yeah, yeah, I just- I just want you to know-"

"What."

"That if the Blue kills us it's all your fault. But I won't be mad."

"Ha, thanks."

"Not like that one time."

17

AFK
Last Month

The cargo plane soared in from the south. We passed over the military base first, an island you could only escape by bridge. Anyone that dropped there might find the heaviest munitions but would have to fight to keep them and then likely spend the rest of the round chasing the Safety Circle across the map. At least ten players decided to take the risk and leapt from the plane.

The first to bail out proclaimed that only real men dropped at the military base and that if you were not a real man you should not bother because you would not survive. This elicited a reaction from a real girl, which was far less common in PBR. The reason for the rarity became apparent as half of the plane attempted desperately to get into her private voice channel. I felt a bit bad for her but promptly forgot as she dropped somewhere in no man's land.

There was still plenty of time to select a drop spot. Speaking of which, The Spot itself was off of the shopping list for that round. The flight path of the cargo plane would force an extended parachute flight just to make it halfway there. I asked Goemon if he was up for some sightseeing but he still had yet to return from the bathroom. That meant I had to make the drop decision for the both of us, to be ready by the time he got back. We would have to choose something further along the path, closer to the northern edge of the island.

The cargo plane passed over the School. The man next to me turned and looked me up and down. He wore a green dinosaur costume, some hybrid of a stegosaurus and a t-rex. The dinosaur's mouth drooped open in a circular cutout with just enough room to expose his face. He opened his actual mouth and told me if we did not drop at school that he would perform unspeakable acts on my mother, and that actually he already had, and that actually the sentiment went for anyone that failed to drop at School. School was the worst, full of endless hallways and dozens of doors with people hiding right behind them waiting for you to turn the knob to an Uzi greeting. The rooftops and the gymnasium were no better. I ignored him and he and his friend dropped out the back along with another fifteen players.

The next major arena on First Island was Polka City. The vast quantity of multilevel buildings provided somewhat of an advantage over the last two spots. You could hang around the outskirts and find some decent loot while the folks in the middle shot themselves to pieces. From there it was as simple as reading the situation, opting to turn tail and run or engage with the remnants of the battle. All in all, a nice balance between heavy action but a decent chance at survival. I would have suggested it myself but Goemon was still in the bathroom. A swathe of players leapt out the back, several of them shouting something in broken English and perhaps Chinese. The plane was beginning to thin out.

There were still a couple of spots left to drop. Sunken City aka Atlantis was coming up soon and we dropped there sometimes. It required careful piloting of the parachute. You simply had no choice but to land on a rooftop. The rooftops had the guns and players up there feasted on those stuck in the waste deep water that flooded the entire city. The variety was fun and I might have picked that one, but the players that dropped had tactical camouflage and berets with medals that implied some kind of special ops experience. They probably would have destroyed us. Good thing Goemon was not back from the bathroom yet.

The gun range was the final stop on the tour, complete with an ocean view. There was nowhere to hide down there, and it all came down to who found what weapon. If you pick up the M16 you are in good shape. If you get the crossbow it's over. Goemon hated dropping there. And he would not have to, because he was still in the midst of the world's longest bathroom break.

I dropped anyways. The only other option was the beach, which held nothing, not even any tasty waves. I figured maybe I could grab some gear and run for it, and Goemon could catch up with me later. I looked back into the plane one more time before jumping out. The only people left were Goemon, still motionless, a slumped over duo dressed in pajamas, and two solos wearing stock gear who had probably never played before and did not know how to exit the plane.

As I plummeted straight down to the firing range, I attempted to gather intel on the competition. Three other duos dropped with me. Because I waited until the last minute to drop, hoping that Goemon would still return, they all had a head start. My rivals landed scattered around the range before I did. I made a last second adjustment when I pulled the chute, steering towards the outer left quadrant where nobody else ended up.

I caught a view of the plane as it exited the map boundary. The system forcibly removed the players still onboard. Goemon, the pajama duo and the two others all fell from the sky out in the open ocean. Their parachutes would deploy automatically, too, but it's not like they had life jackets when they hit the water.

A pile of sandbags served as a display case for the loot I

had available. A pistol sat there asking me to pick it, but I declined. A pistol would never cut it, not against the rest of the firepower located at the range. The only other option was the fabled crossbow: it was terrible unless you landed a headshot. There were five arrows to go along with it. Footsteps marched on the other side of a sandbag wall. They were close, and I had no time to think anymore. I equipped it and loaded in an arrow, a process that took about six minutes longer than it should have.

I climbed on top of the display pile, hoping to get the drop on the other guy. It was a desperate play. The crossbow fired without a sound. The enemy had stopped to pick up something- maybe a vest but I could not tell- so it was as easy a shot as I would get.

"Hey, what did I miss?" Goemon said into the voice chat.

"I'm at the gun range," I said. The shot was good, but I missed the head. I loaded up another one. One more would do it, I figured. Lucky for me the guy had yet to find a weapon. "You're in the ocean."

"I'm drowning. What the heck."

"Can you swim over here please? I need help."

"Honestly, I don't know. I'm about to drown I think."

My target rounded the corner and I chased after him. I was desperate to finish the job. When I made it around myself, I found myself in a narrow shooting lane. At the other end hung a paper target. Between it sat the player with an arrow in his shoulder. Behind him stood his duo partner with an automatic rifle trained on me. I had no vest and no helmet and no chance. I fired the crossbow anyways, and maybe it hit, but I was dead before I got the chance to find out.

18

Loadout

The steep cliffs slowed our descent of radio tower mountain. The trek left us with no time to relax and enjoy the spoils. Most importantly, though, we survived. We would have to loot quickly to make sure we stayed alive.

"You should take the Para," Goemon said.

"Me? Why? I can't hit anything."

"I have the Kar. I'm still feeling it."

"That's true."

"Besides, you're warmed up now. You'll be fine."

"OK. I'll try it."

I already had two weapons in tow, the Mini rifle and the shotgun. I figured I should probably keep the Mini in the event of another long distance encounter. That meant saying goodbye to the shotgun in order to make room for a shiny new power tool, the M249 Para LMG. What did LMG stand for? Don't know, probably lightweight machine gun but that did not make any sense because the thing was ultra-heavy. As in, the heaviest weapon in the game. An UZI was a lightweight machine gun in my eyes. I mean sure my shoulders needed some work and I always struggled with the incline bench press. Ah who am I kidding, my whole upper body could have used a testosterone boost. But the word lightweight just undersold the sheer power that was the Para. Why was it called the Para? Don't know, that is just what we called it in another game.

"Why is it called the Para?" I asked.

"Because, dummy, it's for people who parachute with it."

"Dummy?"

"Yeah."

"Who could parachute with this thing? It weighs 900 pounds."

"Dunno. The armor is all toast. We can't use anything here. At least we got the Para."

Much like there was One Ring to rule them all, I now weld the greatest power imaginable in the PBR universe. At least as far as I was concerned. Technically there could have been other Paras elsewhere on First Island, too, but I had never experienced any LMG on LMG action in any round as long as we had played the game. Only time would tell if I would be corrupted by its great power. Good thing I had my faithful ally Samwise Goemon to keep me on the right path.

All I needed was to grab some ammo and we could be on our way. I checked the first guy who had the machine gun equipped, but he only had half a box. 15 measly rounds was an insult to the weapon and would take it nowhere. It was like filling up a superbike with an eighth of a tank of gas. Where was the rest? I checked the next guy and all he had was 7.62mm ammunition. That was fine for Goemon's loadout, but those did nothing for me.

"There's no ammo," I said. "Did you take it?"

"No. What do you mean there's no ammo?" Goemon replied.

"This takes 556. The guy had like 15 bullets, that's it."
"That's weird."

"Yeah, what the heck. I mean I still got one box left over from the Mini but that's not even a full clip."

"Well just conserve it."

"Conserve it? Conserve the Para?"

"What, I don't know."

"You know what this is?"

"What? We should probably go," Goemon said as he began jogging off toward the Safety Circle. I followed after him.

"This is like. Like you drove me to Del Taco for my birthday. You said hey, actually wait. It's also Taco Tuesday. Taco Tuesday at Del Taco, and you drove me there on my birthday and said, hey, I'm going to get you some tacos."

"That was nice of me."

"I'm not finished. So we're there and I order a bunch of tacos."

"Soft or crunchy?"

"I don't know, crunchy."

"How many tacos?"

"It's three for...well, let's just say I get nine tacos."

"That's a lot of tacos."

"That's my point," I said.

"Do you hear that?" he asked, trying to distract me.

"Let me finish. So I've got nine tacos which is awesome! Except, there is only, uh, three hot sauce packets."

"What kind of hot sauce."

"The hottest one, obviously."

"Three packets for nine tacos is not enough sauce."

"Exactly! That's what I'm trying to say, that three packets of sauce is not enough for this machine gun. I mean, you get my point."

"Yeah, now can I listen? I can't tell what direction it's coming from. It's like five feet away from me. Or a mile, the sound in this game, I swear."

I got a bead on it. Footsteps, most likely, and it sounded like they were running alongside us. It made sense, we were all trying to flee the Blue for the safety of the Circle. Only a madman would run headlong into assured destruction of the BWOD.

"They're close, right next to us. I think to the left up in those trees. It's a duo," I said.
"I hear them on the right. Man, my sound," Goemon said.

"What if there's two." It made sense. The trees provided cover to the left. To the right, the other potential duo might just be rounding the hill. From the sound of the footsteps, their views would converge at almost the same time just by the nature of the direction they were headed. It was a recipe for collateral damage.

"Oh no. We don't want to be in the middle of two duos."

"I think we should hide, let them go past us," I said.

"Really? You want to hide? What about the Blue?"

"What about it? We're in the Safety Circle. You never look at the map."

"You're not wrong."

We hightailed it for a tiny sheet metal shack in the middle of the field. Identical structures just like it- really more a shed than an actual residence- dotted the First Island map's landscape at random. They could also be found in every other map in the game, though they were made of different materials: cinder blocks for Desert Island, bamboo for Jungle Island, maybe ice or whatever for Snow Island but we never ended up there. It was difficult to determine what function the shacks served in the grand scheme of the game world. A tool shed with a picnic table out front in the middle of a field or jungle seemed a bit out of place to me. But, it would work just fine for a temporary hideout.

A level one helmet sat on the picnic table, useless. The holographic sight inside, though, fit nicely on the Para. I had to make my limited ammo count, after all. We closed the door and crouched down low, away from the sole window. Unfortunately, said window faced the opposite direction. It blinded us to the action.

Right on cue, the battle erupted. The right hill duo opened fire with a couple of hefty-sounding weapons. They opted for the good ol' spray the whole clip and hope for the best strategy instead of a controlled burst approach. It took the duo on the left a few moments to respond with a counter attack. It was possible they had yet to locate the exact location of the aggressors. Another scenario could be the defending duo had some decent cover in the trees and wanted to utilize it best they could. After a couple of seconds, right duo stopped, most likely reloading after that assault. The left duo now returned fire with the low thump of one sniper rifle, semi-automatic, and something fully auto of their own.

"What the heck was that thing," Goemon asked.

"Don't know. Sounds like an SKS," I answered. A couple of more distinct shots went off, sounding vaguely like something getting sucked out of a tube or a bowling ball dropping into a body of water.

"How do you know that?"

"I don't. You gotta get your sound fixed, man."

The exchange ceased again and the Dude Duo on the right spoke up. "Listen, ladies, we're going to give you a chance here," the player yelled.

"Ladies?" I whispered to Goemon. He shrugged his shoulders.

"Just surrender and maybe, maybe we'll go easy on you," he continued.

"Thank you for the offer! It sounds very nice!" one of the girls shouted. Her voice sounded very familiar, genuine and friendly. It was a strange tone to take for a life or death situation.

"Stop it, Elly, how many times have I told you not to be..." the other member of the lady duo said to her partner before trailing off. Her voice also rang familiar. Plus that name, Elly. I let my head run a bit wild with scenarios that this was the same duo we had run into back at The Spot. "Screw you, dirtbags!" she screamed before sending off a couple of more semiautomatic warning shots. She must have been the one with the SKS. What was her name?

"What was her name?" I asked Goemon.

"What? Who?" he said.

"The girl talking."

"How should I know?"

"You have a better memory than me. They're the same duo from before. At The Spot, remember?"

"You think so?"

"Yes! I'm positive. One of them is Elly."

"Oh. Maybe you're right. That's funny."

"I am right. The other one is named...Nails."

"Nails, huh."

"Yes!" I raised the volume of my whisper as high as the category of communication would allow. This was it! What were the odds of us both ending up here, out of 100 other players. Now that I think about it, probably 2 out of 100 I guess but statistics and probability never spoke to me in a coherent language. The point was, we could save them. We could all work together. Finish the round as a draw, maybe. Find a four seater Dosha and drive off into the sunset. Elly and me in the backseat would exchange info, obviously. Then...who knows where the relationship could end up. I had no marriage plans but maybe if she was the right girl...

The Dude Duo spoke up again. "If you want, I could teach you how to use that thing. Just a heads up, you'll need both hands."

Another volley of gunfire soared in front of our shack. This time it was returned by the other side. The exchange lasted a few moments. I turned to Goemon.

"We have to help them," I pleaded.

"Who?" he asked.

"Who? Who?! Elly and Nails!"

"Oh. Why? We should let them sort it out."

"Because, man. Don't you have a heart. Haven't you ever been in love."

"Whoa, whoa, whoa, pal."

"I'm just saying."

"Ugh. Alright, alright. Then what do you want to do."

"Can you throw a flash?"

"No."

"OK, OK, good point. Let's just wait for them both to start shooting at each other and then we-"

Both duos engaged with each other in a chorus of gunfire. I kicked open the door and bolted out with the Para swinging, all 45 bullets of it. Just like I hoped, the mountainside Dude Duo was in clear view as I rounded the corner of the shack. They were focused on their enemies in the trees, and by the time one of them turned to look at me I already had him in the holo sight. I fired off all 45 rounds in the span of a couple heartbeats. The recoil was stronger than I remembered, but it might have had something to do with how I never stopped forward momentum. Enough of the bullets hit the mark, though, because my target went down.

I kept my finger on the trigger, deaf to the rapid clicking sound that indicated no more rounds to fire. The second and sole standing member of the duo turned his attention to me. I was defenseless, I could not blame him. I probably would have done the same thing. But he should have focused on Goemon. The thunderclap of the Kar sounded off behind me and a cloud of red mist erupted from the enemy player. At least Goemon understood the plan. The girls in the trees did too, because they finished the guy off before Goemon even had a chance to load the second shot in the rifle. I took some damage, but I was still standing. Could not say the same for the roasted duo.

19

Friendlies

"I would have liked to switch weapons first," Goemon said.

"No time. Besides, you did fine. You knocked him."

"The AK might have been a little more effective than shooting one bullet at a time from fifteen feet away. I probably would have gotten the kill."

There went Goemon again, always obsessed with the numbers on the scoreboard. He was a real stat fanatic, that one. He would have boxed out his own teammates in basketball just to make sure he got credit for the rebound. I told him that and he denied it, of course. He called me dramatic and I told him that it was clear he was being the dramatic one, and so I let him know that he would hardly give a second thought to shooting me in the back if it meant the bullet was going to end up taking down an enemy as well, putting another point up on the scoreboard. He reminded me that in all our days playing PBR he had only teamkilled me once, and to remember how many times I had killed him, and before I got a chance to say all of those times were clearly accidents the girls interrupted us with either a well-placed or terrible gunshot that hit the dirt between my feet.

Goemon snapped his rifle towards the source. Meanwhile, I still held mine down. After all this, I could not believe they actually wanted to kill us.

"You finished?" Nails called down from the trees.

"After all this, I can't believe you actually want to kill us," I shouted.

"That's the point of the game, right?"

"How dare you," I said.

"She's got a point," Goemon chimed in. And yet, no one was pulling the trigger.

"We saved you!" I said. "That's got to be worth something."

"Saved us? yeah right. We had those scrubs right where we wanted them," Nails said.

"They did help us," I heard Elly say quietly. Finally I had someone on my side. It just so happened to be the one that I wanted, too. I don't mean "The One," but, maybe, actually, you never know.

Nails gave her a light push and mumbled something inaudible.

"I don't think they're going to shoot us," Goemon whispered to me.

"That's what I've been trying to tell you. Let me handle this."

"Oh great."

"I'll tell you what. We're going to let you go," I called out.

"You're going to let us go? Oh, that's rich. I've got a scope on your head. And besides, you're out of ammo. Click, click, click," Nails said.

"So you do. And my associate here is the best sniper of the season. He's got the Deadly Accuracy badge to prove it."

"What? Deadly Accuracy- what the heck is that?" Goemon said. I shushed him. It was all part of the plan.

"Fine. You want to leave the loot with us? Then, you are free to go," Nails said.

"Leave without looting? Absolutely not," Goemon said.

"Shh, I know. I got this."

"Look, clearly we both want the loot here," I said and waited for a response. They did not give one, so I continued. "We got one kill, you got one."

"Yeah but I knocked the second guy," Goemon said. I put the palm of my hand towards his face.

"So, what's your point?" Nails responded.

"My point is, I'm proposing a temporary truce. We split the loot. Then, we go our separate ways."

Elly and Nails began whispering to each other. "Then what?" Elly yelled. I can't believe she was already thinking about our future together. That was nice of her. Maybe we were more on the same page than I thought. Or, maybe, probably, she was talking more short term. Play it cool, Fieldy, I told myself.

"Who's to say what the future brings? I'm talking about here, now, we cast aside the dedicated, dare I say antiquated, rules of PBR for this one precious moment and we split the loot like civil human beans. I mean, uh, beings."

"Precious moment?" Goemon whispered.

"Shut up," I mumbled.

"How do we know we can trust you?" Elly yelled.

"If Goemon was going to shoot you he would have done so already. I don't have any bullets, like you said."

A few moments of silence ticked by. Then, the two women of the duo emerged from the trees. Both donned matching warpaint, the center point being a black stripe across the eyes, ending at the ears. It really brought Elly's eyes, but she probably looked good in anything. The black paint matched the leather jackets emblazoned in spikes on the shoulders in color.

Nails' defining characteristic was the frag grenade in her hand, extended high into the air for all to see. "Alright," she said, "but if you so much as lift a trigger finger I'll blow you past the desert island."

"Hey, we call it Desert Island too," I said.

"Is that really necessary?" Goemon asked, motioning to the grenade with his finger rather than the barrel of the gun.

"Yeah, come on Nails, cool down," Elly said. "I'm Elly, this is Nails. You are?"

"Actually we've met. I'm Field and this is Goemon," I said. For a moment, my heart sank lower than the Underground Lake. I could not believe she forgot.

"I know," she continued, "we never got your names. I just figured, you know, in case you forgot ours."

"I'd never forget a voice like yours," is what I wanted to say but what I actually said was, "I'd never forget a legs like hers," for some reason. Fortunately Goemon had my back.

"Well, let's get to it then," he loudly proclaimed. It was clear he was trying to throw them off the scent of my idiocy. It worked because they ignored my comment. Maybe the PBR gods had a heart and they never even heard it.

"Legs, huh?" Nails said. I was never lucky.

"You should probably grab this," Goemon said. Ah, my faithful wingman always had the best ideas. Nothing like a nice group activity to break the ice. Looting the eliminated duo fit the bill just fine. The genius of the plan rested in its simplicity. If everyone got distracted enough I would no longer have the chance to say something stupid.

"What is it?" I asked.

"Auto shotty," he said.

"No way."

"Auto shotty sucks this late in the game," Nails said.

"It's got its uses," her partner said.

"Yeah," I agreed. "See, we like to work as a team. Goemon here handles everything from a distance. I take care of all the stuff in the trenches. Close range, long range dynamic."

"We kind of do that too," Elly said.

"Maybe we have more in common than you guys think."

"Or maybe," Nails said, "it's called basic game strategy."

Whatever she wanted to call it was fine. The fact is the SK12 (as we called it) automatic rapid-fire shotgun slid into our team dynamic like crispy French fries into a California burrito. It was terrible at range, there was no arguing with the surly Nails about that. However, because of its proficiency at close range, it complemented Goemon's long-distance specialization more than I wanted to complement our attractive rival. The SK12 looked like a standard assault rifle in hand or on the ground. Shells were loaded via magazine rather than individually, and the eight total rounds it held were enough to clear out anybody hiding behind a doorway or around the corner of a wall.

Part of me was sad to see the Mini go. But I never got anything done with sniper rifles anyways. I slapped the scope from the Mini onto the Para, and shifted the holo sight onto the auto shotty. It was the best loadout I could have asked for, really.

As for ammo, I still had some shells from the beginning of the round. The player we took down had a couple more boxes of shotgun ammo that would be sure to last the rest of the round. He must have been a bit of a pack rat, because his entire inventory was filled with ammunition from every type of weapon in the game. I took the rest of the stash of 5.56 bullets for the Para and began the arduous reloading process. Two boxes containing 60 bullets total was half of what I would feel comfortable with but it was a heck of a lot better than nothing.

"Can't believe you got a Para," Elly said.

"Yeah it's alright I guess," I said. It was way better than alright but I was just trying to act cool. "What did you guys get?"

"None of your business," Nails said. "Come on, Elly, it's time to go."

I checked the game clock and the Blue was set to cruise in any minute. Something told me that Nails had a different reason for wanting to bail out on our double date, though. I looked toward Goemon to help me salvage the situation but he was still elbow deep in the loot backpack.

"We could stay together, if you want?" I half asked.

"We could what?" Goemon said. Turned out he was listening after all.

"Ha! So what, you can shoot us in the back when it suits you? I don't think so," Nails said.

"No, I just figured, you know, four of us working together stand a pretty good chance at survival. Versus, you know, every man, or woman, or girl or whatever by themselves."

I expected a violent verbal response. Instead, Nails just stood there and narrowed her eyes at me so they were nothing but two bright slits in the shadowy warpaint. It was unnerving and I wished she had just insulted my gear instead. Both Elly and Goemon then looked to her for some definitive answer, as if she were the judge.

A distant rumble in the sky ended the silent standoff. Just across the horizon, another drop plane cruised overhead. The flight path would not cross over us. The payload would be close enough to access on foot, but the journey would consume a chunk of time off the game clock.

"That's our cue," Nails said.

"Maybe next time," said Elly.

"Don't try to follow us. It won't end well for you."

"What, The Drop?" I said. "You going to climb the mountain this late? You can't go around."

"Don't need to," Nails said. She stood up from the loot. She checked her weapons over one more time. "There's an entrance to the underground tunnels nearby."

"Oh no," Goemon said.

"That deathtrap?" I added. "It's glitched. Probably haven't even patched it yet."

"Glitched?" Elly said and stopped in her tracks. Nobody liked a glitch death in PBR. Even the most experienced veterans got swallowed up by them from time to time, and it's not like you got a consolation prize when they occurred. The round-ending ones were a bit like sailor's stories of rogue waves. They were mostly real even without a ton of video evidence, and discussed in hushed whispers by those who had been affected by them directly. Some players laughed them off. Those players had never stared into the void.

True PBR vets had friends or at least friends of friends with stories of glitches that snatched victory away from the top five. The range of tales extended to darker depths, the worst of which claimed to swallow up players who would never be seen again. I personally knew a player, well not personally, but my friend did, who had their duo partner disappear off their friends list altogether mid-round due to a hollow mountain glitch.

"Yeah, glitched. Happened to us not long ago. I couldn't play for a week. Basically," I said.

"Come on, Elly, let's go," Nails said.

"You should go. If you want to get yourself vanished."

"Vanished?" Elly said.

"That's right. I saw it myself. Goemon and I both did. I could tell you the safe way through, if you want. Before you go. So you don't die."

"We should at least hear it out," Elly pleaded.

"Oh for the love of- fine, but make it quick," Nails said as she sat back down.

20

Tunnel Snakes
Several Months Ago

The Eastern Bloc aesthetic was apparent in the architecture of all the towns of First Island, both large and small. It was scrawled on highway signs and above cleared out storefronts. It was found in munitions caches and the humble, if comical, engineering feat that was the Dosha. It was also hidden, lurking underground. What good was a Cold War vibe without a little bit of nuclear espionage?

We visited the tunnels one time, and once was enough. There was one entrance that I knew of, but whispers told of an interconnected network of underground passages sprawled out underneath the entirety of First Island. That's not to say it was an efficient form of transportation so long as you knew your way around. PBR was built on the freedom of movement. It requires player adaptation to placement of the Safety Circle. Survival of combat requires cover and sneaking and hiding behind trees or sometimes, a lot of the time, running away. Put yourself in an underground maze and that all goes out the window. Oh, only there are no windows and it is pitch black except for the occasional flickering red emergency light.

"Yeah, we've played the game before," Nails interrupted.

"I know. I'm just setting the stage. It's important," I said.

"We don't have all round."

"OK, OK."

These were all crucial pieces of information that we learned too late. Our logic was sound going into the ordeal. The Drop phase had been unkind to us. We went a little out of the way to hit The Spot right out of the plane. This put us at a time disadvantage. The fact The Spot had no decent weapons except a 12-round stock Vector SMG for Goemon and a double barrel hunting shotgun for myself did not make the gamble pay off. That left us further behind, and playing catch up to the Safety Circle for most of the early phases.

We looted what we could on the outskirts of the more populated areas. We picked up a couple of vests from a field shed and the picnic table out front. Goemon found a helmet on the second story of a barn. All the rifles in the game went into hiding or in the hands of other duos. Engaging anyone else from a distance was out of the question with our current loadout.

So when we found ourselves square in the middle of two other duos, we knew an alternative game plan was in order. It's like the pros always say, playing cold cuts in a duo sandwich without the right gear is a recipe for a ticket to Sogtown.

"The pros don't say that. Nobody says that."

"I've heard 'em say it." I think I was mostly getting that saying right.

"We're screwed. Maybe we can lie down in the bushes and they'll ignore us. Maybe we should just quit the game and give up forever," Goemon said, maybe not in those exact words but it was pretty close. It was definitely implied.

"Nonsense," I said. "What about...there."

A low hill of green earth rose out of the ground. It would have been invisible from the sky, just another unassuming piece of the rolling landscape. It was easy to see from ground level. The green of the hill hung over a cold cement entryway surrounding a metal door.

Goemon had just about finished covering himself in mud and grass. It was an attempt at homemade camouflage. The act of cowardice made me sick. "You make me sick," I said.

"That's not how it happened," Goemon said. "You're nuts."

"Oh really? Then why don't you remind me."

"I just remember saying things didn't look good. And they didn't."

"Can I finish the story?"

"Do you have to?"

"Yes."

Anyways, I picked up Goemon's spongy excuse for a-

"Dude. Really?" Goemon complained.

"OK, OK, I'll stop."

"Is this going to take much longer?" Nails asked.

"It will if I don't stop getting interrupted," I quipped. I took the resulting silence as an invitation to continue.

Anyways, sometime after I finished convincing Goemon but before the bullets started flying in, we decided to take our chances in the mystery tunnel. The door was heavy and rusted near shut. The only reason it opened at all was due to my own sheer strength of will. And also, just strength. As in muscle strength. I'm pretty strong.

Beyond the door, a cement staircase descended into blackness. The decision of whether to follow proved easy. We knew what was behind us. Four-plus rifles with extended mags and tactical stocks and scopes pointed at our backs. In front of us, though, was a hall of wonders that might end in death but also potentially salvation through escape or, dare I say it, riches.

The first red flag came quickly. The lack of a flashlight

and, I am not ashamed to admit this, my own hesitation, caused me to take an immediate dig.

"Take a what?" Elly asked.

"Take a dig."

"I don't understand."

"You know. He took a dig," Goemon chimed in.

"Right. It means I fell. Hard," I elaborated.

"I don't get it."

"It's just something we say."

"Oh...kay," Elly said.

Where was I? Oh yeah. So I take a dig, hard enough to lose some health. On the bright side, I found a blinking red light at the bottom of the stairs. Under the blinking light was a little metal handle and some words in Russian or something. Goemon whispered down at me to see if I was OK. I told him sure, I think I figured it out. So I pulled the handle and the tunnel glowed a hot red, like I opened the flume on some sleeping fireplace coals. It was easier to see now that the emergency lighting system had kicked on, but the red neon bloom made things even more unnerving than the blackness.

The walls were narrow, enough room for a duo to go shoulder to shoulder but no more than that. I never did get claustrophobic so that did not bother me much. The length of the tunnel added some level of unease. It extended far past my field of vision which meant we were going to be spending a lot more time down there than I had anticipated. The main issue illuminated by the flashing red bulb was that someone else had already been down there. More disturbing was they wanted to let us know. They did this by scrawling a personal message on the wall. Actually, on both walls, and a little bit on the ceiling.

The message was clear only in that it showed we had entered the domain of some kind of psychopath. The letters were shaky and long like brushstrokes painted using an offhand. The first I read proclaimed "DON'T" and "IT'S LOOSE" and "DEATH" and "NO WAY OUT." Then a little bit further a fiery drawing caught my eye, scribbled atop the words "WELCOME TO THE VOID." Needless to say the text was sending out some mixed messages. Which one was it, don't come in, no way out, or welcome? There was only one way we were going to find out.

Goemon checked our six as we advanced down the hall. I wielded the double barrel with confidence, and tried to push back the doubt that it would do anything if my target were all the way down the hall. The only thing to use as cover down there were barrels tagged up with exclamation points, skulls and what I think were symbols meant to convey some form of radioactivity.

The air got stale down there faster than an unclipped bag of flaming hot Cheetos. We progressed further and further into the tunnel. I thought it would never end. That's when the smell hit me.

"Was it you? From the Cheetos," Nails said. Elly laughed and covered her mouth. I ignored the insult and continued.

I should clarify that we had been walking for several minutes. The red light had dimmed to a soft glow, enough to see, but not much. About as bright as the flame of a cigarette lighter, I would say. The entrance behind us was no longer visible. So when the sound came rumbling in...

"Sound? I thought you said smell."

There was, uh, both, sound and smell. The sound rumbled in, deep and low at first but then higher. It was animalistic for sure, but it was no animal I had ever heard in my entire life. It was not behind us, that was impossible.

"No way. There's no animals in PBR," Elly said.

"Maybe not in this iteration. But you ever heard of cut content?"

"Yeah, like weapons that didn't make it in the game."

"Not weapons. Monsters."

"Psh," Nails pushed air out of her lips. It registered as feedback on the mic. "Don't listen to him. There were never any animals in this game. Or monsters, for that matter."

"There wasn't supposed to be, anyways, at least not in this version," I continued.

"What do you mean?" Elly asked.

Like I was saying, the demonic roar seemed to be coming from everywhere. I found part of the answer. The ventilation system above our head served as the perfect transmitter. The acoustics of the cement tunnel- or was it a mausoleum?- did the rest and echoed the noise all around.

I felt in the pit of my stomach that something was wrong. Call it a sixth sense if you want to. This was different from the adrenaline rush of a typical PBR engagement. Something was off. The fear was there, but the usual accompanying anticipation had been replaced by dread.

Still we continued deeper down the corridor. The explorer who walked the halls before us became increasingly brazen with his scrawled ramblings. They degenerated from words to solitary letters intermixed with radioactive symbols like the ones on the barrels. The last legible piece of work appeared to be a print of an oversize hand, or perhaps a five-digit animal claw. It could have been the size of a bear's paw, but something about the placement of the fifth digit made it read as a thumb and a humanoid track. The hand or claw print started out clear but smeared red paint or some other liquid across the rest of the hall. Dark droplets dripped down the wall in places that it had been laid on a little too thick. I ran my finger through it and held it up for inspection. The red light made it tough to determine the composition. For some reason a sudden urge welled up in me to put it to my lips.

"What are you doing," Goemon asked. The suddenness in his voice snapped me out of whatever moment I was in.

"I don't know," I said. It was like a spell over me had been broken. I shook it off. "What is this stuff?"

"There's no paint in PBR, if that's what you're asking."

"Oh, man. You think it's blood?"

"Don't know."

A morbid fascination began to take hold. The tunnel compelled me to travel further and further down into its depths. I was pulled along by some magnetism that only grew stronger the deeper we plunged. Forget about turning back to locate the exit. Anything outside of the cavern no longer existed. Even the game clock no longer mattered. I checked it out of force of habit, and the seconds had slowed to a near standstill. Perhaps we had been down there minutes or hours, but the very notion of time behaved differently.

"Of course, by now, I know what you're thinking. PBR was not always a battle royale game. That's common knowledge. It originally had a different title," I explained.

"What? No it didn't," Elly said.

"It's just a rumor. And a dumb one. PBR put battle royale on the map. They practically invented the genre," Nails said.

"A rumor the mods ban people for even mentioning on the PBR forums," I countered.

"Yeah, because it's off topic. Because it has nothing to do with the real game."

"So they say."

"Yeah, they do say. Because there's not so much as a screenshot proving otherwise."

"We found proof. Horrible, nightmare inducing proof."

"Lemme get this straight. Are you saying you somehow

stumbled into an outdated version of the game, where some other player got stuck, and possibly mutated into a horrifying radioactive creature?"

"Those are your words, not mine," I said.

Elly shot a glance at her partner. Clearly this was not a topic the two of them had discussed before.

"What?" Nails shrugged. "I used to lurk the forums back in the day when we first started playing. I might remember somebody mentioning something about it."

"Mhm," I said in triumph. I basked in the glory of the minor victory. Maybe the story would get through to them.

"Well? Are you gonna finish the story?"

Our footsteps were endless just like the hall they marched down. Goemon and I seemed to share this silent compulsion to continue. The only sounds around us were the dull thud of our footsteps pressing on cement, and the haunting unnatural growl of the creature that reverberated through the vents. We did not seem to be getting closer to the source.

The game clock had long since stopped. The only indication that we were not stuck in a loop was the growing moisture in the air. The atmosphere of the den took on a thick, heavy quality not found in any normal area of the game. It felt as though each step was weighed down, almost sticking to the floor. The walls and the ceiling seemed to sweat as much as I did, but I would not feel them this time. Once was enough.

After what must have been several hours, the concrete began to show signs of heavy wear. The further we continued, the more cracked and broken it became. Raw dirt seeped in between the gaps. Pale sand cascaded onto the floor from a long-running gash on the wall.

Then, we reached the end of the hall and a doorway.

The strange part was not that this hallway did indeed

have an end to it and a door leading outside. It was that the whole thing was encased in ice. Not a clean, flash frozen ice, either, but the kind of chunky white stalagmites that form in a thirty year old freezer. Every part of the end of the hall and the door was frozen or snowed in solid. Every part except for the door handle itself, which appeared to remain unaffected by the rest of the environmental takeover.

I reached out for it instinctively. Goemon and I had come this far. We both needed to see what was on the other side. As my hand neared the metal handle, a voice inside of me gave the briefest of hesitations. It was enough of a second thought to delay whatever process was supposed to take place. An entity on the other side of the door, perhaps related to the one inside of the vent, or perhaps even the source of the otherworldly groans, began to pound violently on the metal. The door shook with each strike, sending shard after shard of ice falling to the ground. The blows to the door were accompanied by an escalating howl, much louder now than it had been, louder than anywhere else in the hallway.

Despite any common sense that would have cried danger and destruction, the louder the howling became the more I felt compelled to pull on the handle of the door. I reached closer to it once more. It seemed as though if I did not pull the handle the entire entry would come flying off the hinges by force anyhow.

"Wait," Goemon said, his voice faint and distant despite his proximity to me. He said it again, and on the third repetition I turned to look at him. He looked pale and ghostly even amongst the white of the strange snow. "Don't open it," he continued.

At that, the entity from the other side wailed as though it were in immense pain. It began scratching and hammering at the door in desperation. I knew if we did not turn away at that very moment then we may never have the opportunity again. I summoned all of the will I could muster and turned around, placing one foot in front of the other again and again until walking felt natural once more.

The way back was far shorter than the way in. It took mere seconds to find the initial stairwell, a sight I must say was greater than any vista or wonder I had ever laid eyes on before. I sprinted up the stairs, Goemon following close behind.

When I opened the door, sunlight and fresh air hit me like smelling salts. Waves of fear and anxiety washed away, and I fell to my knees in the grass. As it turns out, there were two duos outside in the midst of a firefight. Another wave washed over me, this one full of high caliber ammunition, and I never got the chance to find out who won.

21

Bridge Crossing

Nails did not look back as she stormed off. "Alright, that's enough time of mine you've wasted," she said. "Come on, Elly. Let's go."

"You're not seriously going to go for The Drop, are you?" I asked. They had already begun the trek in that direction, which was enough of an answer. I was hoping my knack for dragging things out had ruined their chance at going for The Drop, but she was determined. "You can't go this late in the round."

"Or?" Nails called back. They were about to turn the corner of the road, and thus, take the offramp exit of our highway of love forever.

"Just let them go," Goemon said. "They know what they're doing. Or, they don't. But you know we can't stay together."

"The last Safety Circle will be on the island!" I called out. "You'll have to make it across the bridge, it's a suicide mission!"

"Ha, Safety Circle. You guys are funny," Nails laughed in the distance.

"See you in the lobby," Elly yelled back with a wave.

"Wait! What do you call the Safety Circle! What lobby!" I

shouted.

"They're gone, man. Let them go," Goemon said as he put a hand on my shoulder.

"I just…I love her man."

"Love her? Which one?"

"Which- How dare you. Elly!"

"Oh, right."

"I can't believe she's out of my life, forever, again."

"Mhm. Grab some of this first aid, will you?"

"Yeah, I guess."

"Ah, come on. Things aren't so bad. You've got a Para. And an auto shotty. And there's only twenty people left."

"Yeah, but there's only ONE girl left for me. And now, she's gone."

"Brother."

"OK. You're right. Besides, Elly would want me to continue. We have to stay strong."

"If that's what it takes. You ready to move on?"

"From Elly? I don't know if I ever will, buddy. I don't know if I ever will."

"No, from this spot."

"Oh, yeah. Let's see here," I said, opening up the map. The Blue was headed our way again, faster than I expected. Guess I chatted for longer than I thought. The size of the Safety Circle was getting smaller and smaller in comparison. "Hm. The Circle is going to end up on the island."

"Island? Like the warmup round?" Goemon asked.

"No not that island. The bigger one. You know, the military base."

"Oh, you mean Military Base."

"Yeah. We should probably cross the bridge before it gets too late."

"Now you're talking," Goemon concurred.

"I really don't think they're going to have enough time."

"Well, not everyone has your advanced meta knowledge of the best strategies of Circle survival."

"Wow. That's really nice of you to say, man."

"Sure."

"At the risk of eroding all of the trust you have in my planning ability, I should tell you that there's no way we are going to make it on foot."

"Oh no."

"But I've already found a solution."

"Oh no."

"It's a motorcycle. A two-seater, built for speed."

"Oh no."

The two-wheeled ticket to freedom rested behind a poorly rendered bush. But the jagged shrub could not contain our motorized salvation. The fact it was upright and parked with some attention to detail meant it had somehow gone undiscovered and undriven for the entirety of the round. The model was an off-on road hybrid with knobbier tires and elevated clearance in the front. This was useful in the event of a crash landing off of a stray jump. Any time airborne on a motorcycle was dangerous so any design choices to give an edge of survival were welcome. The bike was jet black from fuel tank to fender. The other motorcycles in the game with yellow paint jobs looked kind of cool but stuck out worse than I did at a house party. The black finish would suit the stealth run across the bridge much better.

"I'll drive," I said.

"Oh no," droned my partner. It was like he was caught in a loop.

"You're so dramatic. It's not like you would rather drive."

"You're right."

"Then saddle up, partner."

The bike roared to life at the insistence of my hand on the throttle. At the same moment, the Blue engulfed us, muffling the noise of the engine.

"You didn't tell me it was that close," Goemon said.

"I didn't realize," I winced. The pain of the Blue would not press past the adrenaline for at least a few seconds. By that time, we would be well into the safety zone.

I opened up the gas and almost lost control. The bike was floaty in the steering department but responsive on the throttle. I knew from personal experience the brakes worked just as well. Too well. It was better to lay off the gas than hit the brakes unless you wanted to go head first into a tree trunk. The helmets in PBR might have helped against the small caliber bullets but they did nothing against high speed collisions.

I held on tight enough for the fishtail to correct itself and peeled out down the road. The Blue Wall of Death was in sight, maybe a couple seconds ahead. We gave chase with the same determination that the Blue did, but had the advantage of two wheels powered by 65 million year old fuel.

I laid off the gas for a moment when we burst through and the damage stopped. Pressing forward was necessary. We had the speed to outrun but any sort of break would place us right back in the deadly tide. It was a delicate dance to perform. Drive too slow and get enveloped by the choking, formless entity. Too fast, go off a bump and into the certain death of a cement wall.

Those were just the dangers if we were playing on the

map all by our lonesome. But PBR was not a driving sim. The handling of the bike and the physics of forward momentum made sure to remind me of that. Basic comprehension of safe motorcycle propulsion was necessary to keep you alive. You had to avoid the scenery, but sometimes the scenery came after you.

It sounded like the bike backfired. Goemon yelled in my ear, asking me what the noise was. We both knew what it was because the engine was running just fine. I told him it was a gun, a sniper rifle, probably, unless somebody decided to try firing a single shot out of their AK at us. That was not true, of course. But on the plus side, the shooter was far away based on my read. On the negative side, we were headed straight towards them.

One of those flat fields spread across the middle of the map would have been nice. It would have been great to be somewhere we could pour on the speed, where the hills were too far away for any enemies to have a good angle on us. But we were headed for the coast, a cluttered area full of towns we needed to avoid and canyons we could not.

"I think he's in front of us," Goemon said.

"I think you're right."

That would make the angle even more difficult for Goemon to land the shots needed to take the other guy down. Realistically, my wingman would not be able to land any. That's not to say it was his fault, either. He was a crack shot, no doubt, but shooting from the hip on the back of a bike at something more than eight feet away was impossible. The only way to survive was to drive.

I considered opening up my map for another way around, but taking my eyes off the road for even a second would spell the end. A master of the craft might dip into the town alongside our currently traveled road, slicing up open lanes between rusted out cars and alleys. I was not that master.

"Hang on!" I yelled.

"Oh no."

I opened the throttle fully and weaved from side to side in the middle of the road. The stone hill on which the sniper laid prone was a recognizable landmark. It butted up to the cliff face of the shoreline. The only way up was a path on the left hand side of the hill. If we maintained speed, banked right, and managed to keep the bike up on both wheels we could blow past them before they would have a chance to follow. From there it was just a prayer that no one would be waiting on the bridge.

At that speed, a single pothole would have sent us off the motorcycle, into orbit, over the sniper's hill and all the way back down into a horrible bone-crunching demise into the rocky depths below. A single squirrel probably would have done the same. For reasons of game balance, bullets in PBR lacked the same stopping power against players in vehicles, off-road motorcycles included. So I watched my health fall off in chunks, but I kept my hand on the throttle. Either the sniper switched to something fully automatic or he had a team-mate up there spraying alongside him. A headshot would have knocked me both literally and figuratively. A single shot to the tire would have likely spelled the end for our duo as well. Instead, I soaked up the bullets with grit and Kevlar and made the turn.

"What is happening?" Goemon yelled. He fired a burst up at sniper rock. Maybe it was covering fire, maybe he actually had a clear shot, my goal was the same regardless. Speed. Nothing else mattered, except for the rust bucket of a Dosha on the side of the road I swerved to avoid. I corrected again, regaining balance, the gunshots behind quieting down and landing in covered ground. My instincts or the adrenaline or maybe even destiny had taken over, like I was having an out of body experience. Only when I glanced at my health did I suddenly recall that I was not invulnerable.

"I need to heal," I said.

"What? Now?"

"I don't know. I mean one more hit and I'm done."

"I'm hurt, too."

"Before or after the bridge?"

Goemon had to answer fast. Once we entered the fabled bridge the only way out was through a body bag or out the other side. With enough distance between us and the aggressors behind, I took my hand off the throttle in preparation.

"Before, I guess. In case there's someone waiting."

The proposition was awful either way. Head onto the bridge with nothing but a sliver of health and a single stray shotgun pellet would end the round. Take too long to heal, and everyone trying to cross the bridge to reach the rapidly shrinking Safety Circle would converge on us. I agreed with Goemon, though. We did not know what was in front of us, across the bridge. But we knew what was behind, and it was a threat we could hide from.

I engaged the brakes slow, and kept the bike facing towards our destination. Rust eaten cars littered the entrance. Two sandwiched together formed decent enough cover from threats on either side. Still, a firefight at that location would be the worst case scenario. If we got bogged down there we would get chewed up by the Blue even if we did survive the engagement.

First aid was still plentiful in the inventory. That was one less thing to worry about. The problem was the time it took to use it. There was no avoiding it though. We would need all the health we could get for the final stretch. After the initial heal, I stared at the bottle of painkillers needed to get up to max.

"Don't forget the painkillers," I reminded Goemon.

"I was thinking of saving them."

"Don't. Might not get another chance."

"Fair enough."

I peeked over the car down the length of the bridge. There were probably a dozen more piles of scrap metal all the way down. Any one of them could hide an opportunistic duo looking to poach someone late to the party. Fortunately, we were not the only ones looking to cross the bridge.

22

The Dance

The SUV that rumbled towards the bridge took us by surprise. It should not have. Based on the previous encounter with Elly and Nails we had hard evidence that several duos still remained outside the island of Military Base. We were not the only ones desperate to reach the final stages of the Safety Circle, and we could not be the only ones who hated the bridge.

The auto shotgun was a possibility if the SUV got close enough, and it looked like it might. I could also get lucky with a fully automatic spray down courtesy of the Para. Goemon could peek and line up a headshot with the Kar, maybe. He had that scope, after all.

Instead, we made a silent agreement to hold. No need to go all in anymore with the finale so close and this was not the prize. The scoreboard placed us in the top 15 still alive. We had the guns, we had the ammo, and we had the armor, bullet-ridden as it was. But it did not mean we needed to use them. At this point in the game, stealth was just fine.

The tactical goal was to stay behind the other players, but inside of the Safety Circle. This strategy would become more important the smaller the Circle got. The Blue made for the best camouflage, but it did no good if you could still get shot in the back.

Goemon went prone and stared through the scope underneath our rust bunker of a car.

"These guys are coming in hot. I don't think they know we're here. Or they don't care," he said. "I think I- hey, I'm pretty sure I see those girls, they're on foot."

The SUV, meanwhile, roared past without letting off the gas. There were multiple reasons for passing us by. It was possible we stayed hidden, they were scared or under equipped at this stage, or they could have been desperate to make it to the Safety Circle before it was too late. Whatever the reason, they were going too fast to navigate the obstacles of the bridge.

I checked the map to see how far away The Blue Wall of Death was from our position. We still had some time to spare to see how the bridge would play out. If Goemon was right about Elly and Nails and they were already stuck in the Blue, things looked grim for them. My own scope showed me nothing but a featureless duo in a full on sprint through the death wave. It was a bad way to go. Part of me hoped it was some randoms. The other part wanted it to be them, with the caveat that they somehow survive.

But there were more pressing matters than dwelling on the potential plight of my future ex-girlfriend and her evil partner. The speeding SUV hit something on the bridge, and then crashed into something else, and in the midst of playing pinball became the target of some heavy arms. I turned around just in time to watch the car erupt into a fireball before catapulting over the top of the bridge support beams. Lucky for the players within, the icy water beneath the bridge put the fire out. According to the scoreboard, though, they were cooked and it was down to the top 13.

"What in the world gun was that?" Goemon asked.

"Don't know. Grenade, maybe? No, I feel like we definitely would have heard someone yell 'Kobe.' Plus that was an impossible throw."

"Scoreboard says...C4. Wow. People are getting serious. I have literally never used it."

"We've been missing out! This whole time!" I laughed. Of course, the laughter was just to contain my own fear. Sure, it would have been fine and dandy to use C4 effectively. But I didn't really care about that. The fact was that SUV bit the bullet big time for us, and they had no idea. If we did not stop to heal, we would have sped across the bridge and exploded in their place, clearing the way for them. Had the timing changed by a couple of seconds we would be dead. If the players on sniper rock had been worse shots, they would have missed us, we would not have stopped to heal. The whole concept of a PBR round was so fickle. The longer we survived, the longer I thought that you had to have fate on your side in order to win. Did it really all come down to randomness? Was there anything we could really do? Or was I just so scared of taking personal accountability that I was ready to blame someone, anyone else for a failure that had yet to even happen? Nah, no way that was it, we were in the Round of Destiny.

"I guess so. It's not automatic though, right?"

"I don't think so. I think you have to trigger it."

"That means somebody is watching and...there they are."

The victorious C4-wielding duo of the bridge had turned tail. They were currently en route to the Safety Circle, or at the very least headed in that direction. They had to know other duos would be crossing the bridge, whether it was us or someone else, so why would they abandon their post? Could be as simple a reason as they were out of C4, but likely it was that the Blue Wall made cowards of us all. I was no exception to that rule, but the question became how we would proceed across the bridge.

"Bike or foot?" I asked Goemon.

"Foot. I don't want to explode. We'll just get shot off the

bike anyways."

"Not if I drive fast enough. Besides, they're not even facing us."

"I think they'll probably turn around if they hear the engine."

"I can't believe you don't trust my driving."

"Let's just go already."

"I just don't know if we'll make it. But, fine, if you want to die by the Blue then let's die by the Blue."

"You are out of control, do you know that? There, I'm on the bike, are you happy?"

"Yes."

"Can we go already?"

"Yeah, hang on one sec."

"There's two duos behind us. One in front. The Blue is about to come in. You want me to hang on."

"Yeah exactly," I said. I jumped off the bike and moved to the middle of the roadway. I took one last glance through the scope towards the friendly duo in the distance. The very concept of friendly in PBR should not have existed at all. As long as the round continued, Elly and I could never really make it work. There were no ties in PBR. Eventually, one of us would have to pull the trigger. It could be me or it could be any other random player. The shot would have been good enough, even at that distance, even with the Para. They made no attempt to find cover or to run any kind of evasive pattern. They lacked the time. The BWOD was taking its toll. It waited for no one. I lowered the gun, reached into my inventory and left three first aid kits in the center of the path. I would have left a note if I could.

"OK. Let's go," I said and jumped back on the bike.

"What if the other duo gets it?" Goemon said.

"I don't know man. I had to do something."

If Goemon said something it was inaudible over the roar of the bike. My little charity stunt might have eased the guilt I felt at leaving Elly behind. At the same time, it caused me to lose track of the duo across the bridge and that felt almost as bad. I knew well enough that the enemy duo were the toll watchers, and if they abandoned their post then the rest of the bridge was free and clear of players. This allowed for full concentration on the obstacles of the road, at least until we crossed back into enemy territory.

Loot crates were the only remnants of the exploded SUV. They joined three others and the accompanying lifeless players. Guess the bridge watchers had been busy, and successful. We had neither the time nor the need to stop and check the contents of the crates. Instead I hit the gas, splitting two burning barrels, swerving left to avoid a Dosha and then right again to dodge a dilapidated pile of wheels and scrap. The process felt a bit like navigating a tombstone covered graveyard, only at breakneck speed and without the bad karma.

The bridge's exit marked a turning point. The final phase of the round was upon us, and we attacked it with full force. Whatever happened on the other side of that bridge- the looting, the loving, the killing- no longer mattered. The only thing that mattered now was hanging on, to the bike, to the guns, to our lives.

"Where are they?" Goemon asked.

The way I figured, the Bridge Watcher Duo had three options. The gas station to our immediate right provided cover and a lone window to shoot out of. The guard tower on the hill at 45 would be a logical place for sniping, but my instinct for timing said if they picked that one we would be able to see them running up the side. The last option was through the trees, for natural cover while marching towards the Safety Circle. Of course, there was also the road dead ahead but they would have to be insane to stay exposed like that.

"Don't see them," I replied. We cruised past the gas station. No gunshots. "Do we just drive straight to the base?"

"Might as well, I guess. At least the outskirts."

The patch of forest would be a death trap for the bike so our only choice was the road. It banked right and sloped up just enough to obscure whatever lurked on the other side. Countless other rounds in that exact location seared the landscape in my memory. It was the final high point before the slow descent toward the fortified Military Base.

We crested the slope and the front tire exploded as soon as I caught sight of the Bridge Watcher duo. I lost complete control of the bike as it took a ninety degree turn to the left. It turned into a bucking bronco ride that I no longer had control over. The only way to win the game was to hang on tight and slow down when we hit the trees. It occurred to me that I hoped we would not literally hit said trees.

Somehow we managed to stay upright amidst the janky turn and the uneven ground, and when we stabilized enough Goemon returned fire.

"They're in the ditch. I got an angle," he yelled.

The way the bike bounced and swerved made us the tougher target to hit by far. That did not stop the other duo from trying. But they had no discipline. Both of them sprayed in a wild, uncontrolled fashion, landing nothing but a few hits to the bike. The shots to the motorcycle must have been unintentional. It took somewhere above a full magazine of bullseyes to blow up a vehicle by force in PBR. Pebbles and logs were the things to watch out for, and we were about to find plenty of both.

"We're going to have to bail," I said as the woods approached. A moving dismount was suicide. We had to stop to jump, which would also leave us vulnerable. Goemon had to buy us some time. He did.

"I knocked him. I can't believe I knocked him. It was my last bullet," he yelled, reloading.

That was the edge we needed. "Get ready to jump," I shouted and slammed on the brakes. The solo standing member of the opposite duo was either reloading himself or trying to pick up his teammate. Either way, it gave us the two seconds or so we needed to ditch the bike and jump behind a tree.

My heart pounded, and my vision narrowed into a blurry tunnel. Goemon and I looked at each other and nodded. I stared down the scope of the Para and leaned around the trunk of the tree. The fools were both crouched in the ditch with no cover from the waist up. I hardly minded that both of them were back in action. It just gave me more chances to land shots. I pulled the trigger and held fast, determined to dump out all of my ammo reserves if I had to. Forget about discipline. That all went out the window when you had close to a hundred rounds to burn through. The first went down in a show of crimson vapor. I decided to forget the scope, snapping my aim over to the next one from the hip instead. Maybe I missed fifty bullets, so long as I kept shooting it did not matter. In another second the enemy player ragdoll collapsed and the engagement was over. I began the reload process immediately.

"Whoa," Goemon said. "How many bullets did you just shoot?"

"All of them," I said.

23

Time To Choose

Top 11 and two more frags on the scoreboard. To be fair to the Bridge Guardian duo, they did not stand a chance against the Para at that range. The midrange might as well have been Para town, population me, or something like that. They took a trip on the Para train. Yeah, that was good too. Either way, I was definitely mayor, or I guess conductor. Point was, they were in no man's land, with no cover and nowhere to run. Besides, they had every opportunity to take us down. They just lacked the skills to finish the job. Popping a tire was one thing. But when you have the Round of Destiny on your side, it will take a lot more than that to-

"Dude," Goemon said. "You should probably heal."

"Oh. Yeah."

I still had one more first aid kit left over from my generous, and anonymous, no less, donation to Elly. While I patched myself up, I wondered how they were doing. We had a head start with the motorcycle for sure, but they would likely be at the bridge by now and picking up that crucial health. I opened up the map to check the position of the Blue.

My heart sank. The Safety Circle had jumped away from us yet again, smack dab in the middle of the military base. We were not far. We would make it. But we would have to hustle. And the no man's land that trapped our opponents in the last engagement would be nothing compared to the fortified outskirts of the base. The sooner we left, the better.

"Top 11, Circle's at military base. Para, sniper rifle. We're gearing up for a photo finish, here," I said. "The Blue's coming in but if these guys had health I think we might have time to wait for Elly and Nails and still make it."

"Top 11? Try Top 8."

I checked the scoreboard. Three more had perished in the midst of our firefight. The heaviest casualties in PBR always took place at the beginning of the round. There was no question there. But as the Safety Circle shrank, the battleground did too. The skirmishes happened with more frequency, with the added caveat of far deadlier weapons. Nor did the Blue Wall of Death take any prisoners. It made me wonder.

"Did you catch the names of the last three who died?" I asked.

"No."

"It's just. Sounds like a duo and a half died, all at once."

"Yeah."

"Elly and Nails probably would have ran into the rock sniper duo at the same time they were all crossing the bridge."

"Oh...yeah. That would make sense," Goemon said. He must have sensed a loss in focus brewing under my skin. "But, you know, I'm sure they're fine, we'll probably see them at the finale."

"Yeah, probably," I agreed, a flat-out lie to myself and to Goemon just to try and play it cool. I had to play it cool. This was the end, the time to choose between finally being better than everyone else at something for once or a slumped over failure. It was harsh but true. Maybe too harsh, I never did work well under too much pressure. It had to be just the right amount. "Let's just have fun," I said, another lie to myself to try and calm down a bit.

"I'll have plenty of fun looking back on this if we win."

It was a sentiment I could agree with. We were close to the Safety Circle, close to winning, close to achieving that elusive recognition that came with the territory. But to win we had to live, and to continue living we had to move.

"Right. In that case, let me grab a first aid kit from these guys and we can roll."

"Just take mine. I got a couple. No need to stop and get shot by whoever's still behind us. We can cut through the forest."

"Cool, thanks buddy."

This was the final stage of the game. Ammo and first aid was often plentiful, and this round was no exception. We just spent in game hours searching toilets and tool sheds for every item we needed or did not, and the fact was most of them would end up unused in the bottom of the backpack. We had earned our invitation to the dance. My new date, because my old one was either dead or going to end up trying to kill me, was destiny. I had no choice but to say yes to the proposition.

"Will you be my chaperone?" I asked Goemon.

"Your what?" he said.

"I don't even know anymore."

"Maybe you need a break."

"What I need is a win, just as bad as you."

"Oh, YEAH. Let's go, baby."

It was as close as we would get to a rallying cry, and we should have saved it for the edge of the forest. To tell the truth, the forest was not much of one. Most of the current tiny island had been cleared out by the military base and the roads leading up to it. The trees remained likely due to the rocky, unusable patch of land they somehow grew out of. Resilient creatures, they were. Maybe we could take some inspiration from them.

We pushed through them without issue. Another clearing greeted us, this one being far more deadly. Between us and Military Base, us and the Safety Circle, was nothing but flat grass and two sets of chain link fences maybe twenty yards apart from each other. The distance between the security of the trees and some semblance of cover behind a silo or a standard issue bunker was tough to gauge. For sure it was more than feet, less than kilometers, and probably about an eight second run. It was impossible and necessary to march across the territory. It was also insane. With no cover and most likely all nine people still alive and already inside, probably teamed up, definitely with their guns pointed right in our direction, we would never make it. The good news was the grass had no mines in it, so at least we were guaranteed to keep all of our limbs.

"We run out there, we're dead," Goemon said.

"We gotta go. Gotta risk it. The Blue is closing in. We can still make it to cover inside the Circle before it does."

"We won't make it to cover because we'll be dead."

"But we'll be dead if we stay here."

"The Blue won't kill us right away."

"So?"

"So, we follow it into the Circle."

"Mm. Take some damage, trade off as cover."

"Exactly."

"I hate staying in the Blue."

"Yeah well getting shot is worse."

"True."

"Here. We should drink some energy drinks."

"Always a good idea. Cheers."

I pounded the drink as the Blue Wall of Death enveloped us. It was less a warm hug and more an iron maiden. The feeling was immediate, sort of like a seatbelt engaged too tight in an emergency braking procedure, only this one never let up unless you got out of the Blue.

Goemon crouched and I did the same. We moved slower that way but we matched the pace of the Wall almost exactly. With the battleground being as small as it was, the Blue no longer needed to operate at such a high speed. It was nice of the devs to implement one quality of life feature at least, so I could lumber along and spend as much excruciating time inside the BW as possible.

Vision from inside the Blue was obscured, but we could still see out. It was about the same as staring through a tinted window. It was much worse for the players on the outside looking in. They could still see us if they looked at the same spot long enough. But their vision would have to fight through environmental effects like swirling clouds and forked lightning and the general darkness that took place inside the moving storm that was the Wall. For them, it was like staring into a dim night without the benefit of adjusted eyes.

We could not lurk within the Blue forever. I had a hard time concentrating on anything other than my own health bar, ticking down like the remaining seconds on the phase clock. The energy drink slowed the process, but did not plug the leak entirely. I should have been scanning the Safety Circle for enemies. Hopefully Goemon was able to remain more focused than I was.

The Blue crawled to a stop, designating the boundary of the arena for the next few minutes. I figured based on the size of the Safety Circle we had entered the penultimate phase, although I was not as familiar with the range of the battleground at the final phase as I should have been. Best estimation put the Circle at the length of a football field compressed into a ring.

It might shrink two more times, three more, maybe it could go down to the size of a bedroom. I did not know. The only way I could find out was to escape the choking grip of the death cloud.

"When are we getting out of here," I said. There were plenty of decent hiding places from my perspective. The Safety Circle had selected a cluster of buildings as its arena, most of them small and single story. Probably barracks, I figured. A three story number in the middle I recognized as some kind of central communications tower. Two guard towers nearby sat empty. They were death traps at this point. A broken wall stretched around the perimeter between us and the buildings.

"In a minute."

"I'm dying. I'll be dead in a minute."

"Cool your jets, you have two-thirds of your health left."

Gunfire erupted from one of the barracks. It was difficult to tell which. It might have even been several of them at once. Goemon might have spotted something I did not, because he took off out of the Blue without a countdown. He could have at least said "Now." I hustled behind and felt the immediate decompression of my chest. It was nice to be able to breathe again, especially in the midst of an all-out sprint.

Goemon landed on the near side of the wall and hit the deck. He chose a spot with no massive holes nearby. It was a purely defensive move. We would not be able to see any enemies on the other side, but they would not be able to see us either. It did not surprise me that he scoped up facing the Blue, away from the sound of action. We might not be the only ones making a break for it. Though, there were not many others left.

I crouched down next to him and aimed the Para at the Blue Wave of Destruction. No movement, not even from the death cloud itself, but there were only two potential sources of attack on our position. One was the theoretical sole survivor of the battle all the way back on the other side of the bridge, Elly or Nails or the rock sniper boys. If they somehow survived that much time in the Blue they would still be headed out of it any second. The only other exposure point was on the other side of the wall. They could jump through one of the several gaps in an effort to get out of whatever firefight was going on just on the other side, and it would put them right on top of us.

The gunfire ceased, at least for the moment. I checked the scoreboard. Still eight people left. It was probably three duos and two singles if all of our guesses held up right. From the sound of it everyone was tucked away in a safe spot. That would change just as soon as the Safety Circle started its next eviction process.

24

Circle

"Now what do we do?" I whispered.

"We wait," Goemon said.

Then it was radio silence. And not just for us, either. Every man, woman and child in the server, all of the pack rat looters, the sharpshooters, the tactical geniuses, the just got luckies of the round- all of the survivors- were within shouting distance of each other. It did not matter how we or any of our adversaries got here. This was the final battle, and everyone was waiting for someone else to make the first move.

It was in this silence that every ambient noise of PBR made itself known. Listening had never been more important. A single footstep on barracks tile, a reloading magazine, a brushing of denim against a wall would be enough to alert someone to a location. I could hear none of this. Other sounds flew in from every direction. A bird chirped at 65. I kept my composure enough to remain stationary instead of flicking the Para towards it. I had heard plenty of birds but I had never seen a single one in game. Wind rolled through the trees at 120, shaking its branches gently like a slow maraca. The creak of a door groaned at 90, but without any responding gunfire it must have been my imagination. Then there was the constant drone of the Blue Wall of Death. It bore a resemblance to industrial machinery behind a sealed warehouse. It did not assault the ears, but it was also impossible to tune out completely. It was a lovely reminder of our own most likely inescapable and impending demise by way of dry drowning suffocation.

Then I heard something else. Something that was not ambient, but an outsider in the environment. It was nothing more than a slight shuffling sound, maybe fabric rubbing against fabric. But it was close. If my ears were correct, the sound was emitted from just on the other side of our cement cover wall. Someone, or even possibly a duo, was using the other side for cover. Unless they could hear my heartbeat- which, judging by its current tenacity, they might be able to- my gut said they had no clue we were on the opposite side of the wall. We were back to back, with the exception of the foot of cement between us.

I switched over to the auto shotty. At that range, there was simply nothing better. Equipping it into my hands triggered an innate reaction calling for me to leap over the wall to end whoever was there before they got wise to our location. I cast the urge aside. I might get the kill if they were facing the other direction. I mean I definitely would. But I would also guarantee my own death at the hand of Wall Guy's partner or any of the other players waiting for their opportunity to shoot. Besides, Goemon would never go for that. We still had time on the clock before the Blue rolled in again. Not much time, but there was no need to force our hand at that specific moment.

Goemon and I looked at each other. I nodded. It was a silent attempt to let him know we were both on the same page and I was not going to do anything stupid. His eyes got wide and he shook his head. I nodded harder. It just caused him to shake his head harder. I think we were having some kind of difference in opinion or maybe just a communication breakdown. I tried again. This time I tapped my wrist as if I were wearing a watch and shook two fingers towards the wall. He took a hand off his rifle and placed it on his forehead before bringing it down over his eyes. I was starting to think he did not trust me, but I don't know how he got that idea. We made it this far. I was being good.

Restrained, even.

Before I got the chance to explain with more detailed charades, the player on the other side acted. He had a sniper rifle judging by the whip-crack that shattered my ears. At first I wondered if it was the Rock Sniper from before, and he somehow managed to sneak both around and in front of us without either party knowing. Then I wondered why he still had the sniper rifle equipped at this close quarters of a battle. His shot was not at us, because he was still on the other side of the wall. I had no view or way of knowing whether he landed it, but whoever he aimed at did not return fire. The Wall Guy/Maybe Rock Sniper was prone judging by the sound he made as he retreated backwards along the cement wall. He was crawling across the floor.

There were several items to take away from the lone shot fired. First, this was confirmation that Wall Guy possessed no knowledge of our position. He would not have shot at someone else if he knew we were right behind him. He was also either solo or separated from his duo partner because he was both the only one who fired and the only one still moving around. Judging by the sound of his awkward crawling back into safety and the direction of his shot, he was facing toward the right. There were gaps in the wall on either side, so if we entered on the left he would never be able to turn around in time to defend himself. Finally, the barracks on the other side of both the wall and Wall Guy must have been empty. If a duo were hunkered down inside, they would have annihilated Wall Guy through the window. If they waited, they would have lost any advantage. Sure, we waited, but we had a wall between us and the knowledge we were the furthest duo on the fringes of the battlefield. The only unknown I could figure was why Wall Guy had chosen to remain outside the building if it were unoccupied. Maybe he just had no time when the shooting started.

I wanted to sit down and get Goemon's detailed opinion on the whole thing. I wanted to see if maybe he had the same reads as me. To see if he thought the best course of action was to jump right over the break in the wall, blow away Wall Guy and take refuge in the empty barracks where we could await our next move. We did not exactly have that luxury.

The Wall Guy decided to try his luck again. He inched along the other side of the barrier like a snake through the grass. I was certain everybody else in the arena had eyes on his position, and they were just waiting for him to peek around the corner of the barracks. It also meant they all had eyes on our position, but hopefully they lacked the intel that we were behind the wall.

Wall Guy reached his sniper spot again and he fired. This time, his target fired back. It sounded like a couple of players did. Poor Wally tried to shuffle back into his cocoon, but he was too slow to make it back in time. The flurry of rifle fire cut him down and knocked the total of players remaining down to seven. He must have been a solo after all, or the Rifle Duo shooters got a clear headshot. Several bullets hit the concrete wall on the other side of my own head, but I remained steadfast. The wall would hold fine, no need to panic yet. Nobody knew we were there, and the last obstacle to the barracks was removed for us.

We did have to hope that Wally had no partner left in the game. For starters, if he still had a living partner it was one more person we had to deal with who might be on the other side of the wall. Worse than that, the Rifle Duo would still be trained on that same location that they took Wally down, which might put us in the line of fire when we made our move.

Unfortunately, the time to play out all the potential scenarios had disappeared. In its place rolled in the Blue Wall of Death. I opened the map to check positioning. We were certainly out of the Safety Circle if we stayed on that side of the wall. The barracks might be inside the protected zone but it was tough to tell for sure. It was going to be close either way.

"Blue's coming in," I whispered to Goemon.

"Already?"

"Yeah. It's the end." We still had a few seconds before it would envelop us. I suspected Goemon would want to use the big blue hazard as a cover again. It worked for us last time but I still hated the idea of willingly taking damage.

"I think the barracks is clear," I said.

"How do you know?"

"I didn't hear anybody, did you?"

"No, but they could be hiding."

"Yeah but don't you think they would have killed the guy over the wall?"

"Not if they didn't have to."

"Well we gotta do something."

"Let's wait for the Blue."

"Fine. We going over the wall?"

"Yeah, hopefully we can hide behind the building."

Goemon was more optimistic than I was regarding the size of the Circle. We would find out soon enough. The Blue enveloped us once again, and the two thirds of my health began to dwindle further down in response.

"Let me go first," I said. After all, I had the auto shotty. If anything was on the other side of that wall, I should be the one to handle it. Goemon was happy to oblige, and I vaulted over the gaping crack in the wall. The Blue would help with the noise of our movement, but I hit the ground hard and anybody nearby would have heard my feet slam into the dirt. I looked left along the wall while I cleared it and found no one there. To the right, just the corpse of Wall Guy. At first glance, nobody else could see us from that angle.

"Clear," I called. Goemon was already bounding over the wall himself, AK in hand. Unfortunately, the zone between the cement barrier and the barracks was safe only from other players. The Circle was just beyond our position. The Blue continued to chip away at our health. An alternative option was to burn through the remaining first aid as long as we could, but it was not sustainable. Healing would leave us helpless out there, and we would have to get into the Circle eventually anyways.

"We gotta go in," I said, pointing at the grey metal square of a building. Even if the building was empty it did not guarantee survival. From the map it looked like maybe half of the barracks was within the Safety Circle.

"Yeah, I know," Goemon said.

"I'll take the door, you take the window. Ok, go!" I said.

"Whoa whoa-"

It was too late. I was already at the door, which was fortunate enough to be on our side of the building. The window I failed to actually see, but I figured Goemon would make it work if I ended up needing the help. Mostly I thought that the building would be empty and it would not matter.

My footsteps were still obscured by the drone of the Blue Wall of Death. I kicked in the door and instinct took over. If the player residing inside had been smart they would have chosen behind the door as a good hiding place. People behind the door always got me. Instead, he picked a corner right in the view of my auto shotty which I fired from the hip. I unloaded every shot. The tiny one room building was as good as a lab test environment for the weapon. I had no choice but to hit my target. I took a hit or two as well, but even with my lowered health the damage output of the auto shotty was just too high for the other player to overcome. He might as well have brought a knife to the gun fight.

25

Oh Boy

Goemon used the open door instead of the window. And why would he do anything different, considering I cleared the place out already. He closed it behind him and joined me in my humble corner. The rest of the barracks was empty except for the Blue Wall of Death which had swallowed ninety-five percent of the space inside. I could feel it nip at my heels even though it had stopped advancing.

It was good to be out of the open and out of the Blue, even just barely, but I was in rough shape myself. I had lost more health in the exchange than I would have liked. My frag brought the total down to six to go in the round, but it felt more like five and a half the way I looked.

"I'm hurt real bad, Pa," I said. We were pinned down in the corner of the barracks with no reasonable way out. I began to make peace with the prospect of finishing top six. It had been a long journey, we all grew mentally and emotionally and spiritually, maybe dying was not the worst outcome. Living, winning, was not everything. We tried.

"You're OK," Goemon said, healing his own minor environmental injuries. He would survive. For now.

"Maybe it's not the win. Maybe it's the friends we made along the way."

"Shut up and heal."

"OK."

Goemon made a convincing argument. I grabbed a first aid kit off of the Barracks Guy and healed up. Maybe there was a way out of this thing after all. We didn't walk sixteen miles through pure muck to end this thing now. So the Blue Wall of Death was inside our front door. So the other two duos left were already holed up with better positioning. Who cared if I only had enough Para ammo for one more clip. The point was there were only three duos left, and we were one of them.

The Safety Circle had shrunk down from football field to maybe the size of a basketball court. We were all practically on top of each other now. The other two duos had to know we were in the barracks. But as soon as the BWOD moved in again we would die by the hand of the game. We had no choice but to leave.

"Are we going out in the Blue?" I asked. I already knew the answer.

"We can't go through the window. Won't even make it out."

"When do you want to move?" I said and switched back over to the Para. It was more versatile at different ranges than the auto shotty. More importantly, I needed to finish the round in style.

"As soon as the Blue moves, we move, low and slow," Goemon said.

"Like brisket."

"Sure."

The plan sounded good on paper, much like the very paper that wrapped up said barbecued brisket. But I was not the only one cooking up ideas. The stillness of the air made it easy to hear a clink from the direction of one of the other buildings. I knew it was a grenade immediately, but I did not know the variety. Not like it mattered, we would not stick around to find out. Goemon dipped back into the Blue Wall and headed for the door. I bounded after him. There was no glass left on the window to break, so the grenade had no trouble arcing right through empty space and onto the cement floor.

The ground of the barracks erupted in flames. It caught my leg on the way out of the building, but the damage was not enough to knock me. We were fortunate it was a Molotov cocktail, an explosive grenade would have taken me out for sure.

I ran out into the Blue storm to the sound of heavy gunfire. It all materialized from a distance, with nothing coming from Goemon. He moved back behind the barracks. Deeper into the Blue. It was impossible to pin down the source of the assault while staying alive. Cover was the only option. We could hide in the Wall for a few seconds but we would need to move soon or die to the environment. The biggest issue, aside from the choking cloud and lack of health, was where the shots from Grenade Duo were coming from.

The third duo found the answer, and joined in the fray. A full on firefight broke out between the other four surviving players, all of whom instantly forgot about us. It was all about the pressing issue, and Third Duo ripped the belt away from us at the perfect time.

"One's at 40 I think, the other at 90," I called. The BWOD choked my health to below half. "Pick a spot and I'll follow you, we got to go."

Goemon had a knack for finding the best cover. I picked spots that were too obvious. Anything that looked good to me was a stay away. The guard tower seemed like a great vantage point, one we would immediately get shot in. The barracks looked good to me too and that ended in the floor becoming molten lava and my socks getting burned off.

The other two duos were busy with each other, so the time to close the distance was now. The duo at 40, Third Duo, had taken refuge in a barracks nearly identical to the one that we just fled. I still did not have eyes on the Grenade Duo. Based on the angle they needed to land that Molotov grenade in our old hiding spot and not get destroyed by Third Duo I figured they had to be in the three-story radio tower.

Meanwhile, the Blue had moved in again. What had to be the final Safety Circle was set. There were two buildings inside of its boundary. Both of them were occupied, neither of them by us. It was a fitting start to the end of the match. Goemon and I were the sole team on the outside looking in.

We had no choice but to use it to our advantage. I crept through the Blue alongside Goemon. We slid over towards Third Duo. They were the closer of the two, so we could get behind them faster. The barracks was also smaller, which was a double edged sword. It would be easier to light them up but also easier to get shot down ourselves. If I had a grenade I would have tossed it in there and cleared it out, easy. I never had any grenades.

We paused a half step outside of the reach of the Blue. I caught sight of one half of Third Duo through a window. He was busy tracking somebody in Grenade Duo through the other window. The building had two: a convenient one for me to see into, even if the angle was funny, and one on the adjacent wall that Third Guy aimed through.

"I got the shot. He's in the window. Go around," I said.

Goemon nodded and took a swing pattern to the other side of the barracks, at least as much of a swing pattern as the constrained perimeter allowed. I could wait no longer. I scoped in with the Para and let fly. Something about that funny angle and the position of the scope or the zoom sent the first burst of bullets into the window ledge despite my crosshair being square on the guy's helmet. I managed to correct, but the surprise was ruined. He took a couple of hits before ducking out of sight.

Grenade Duo ceased fire in response. I allowed myself a

glance at the scoreboard to make sure they were actually still alive. Still six left. If they left their post, there was nothing stopping them from heading to my flank and ending me. I held fast anyways, crosshair steady on the window, just waiting for sight of a helmet. My only shot was that Grenade Duo was too scared of abandoning the comfort of their three-story penthouse of a bunker to go out in search of a kill. It was a gamble, but one that I to make.

"I swear I hit him. I swear to everything. But he's not down," I said.

"How did you miss? I thought you had the shot."

"I don't know. My scope was right on him. I'm covering the window. I'll still get him. Go for the door."

Goemon went silent again. If he disagreed he would have said something. The Blue Wall of Death whispered in my ear, an effort by the world to distract me. I would not change my aim. I refused to look anywhere else. I almost had to lock into a mantra. Two duos left. One dead ahead, and soon to be dead altogether. The other was in the tower. If I looked around I would miss my chance and if I missed my chance then the round was over.

Maybe three total seconds ticked by, though it felt stretched out further than my lunch budget. The realization of what was happening dawned on me. The Third Duo was in the corners of the barracks. They were healing. Correction: they were healed by now. I would have to start the battle from scratch, and at a significant positional and health disadvantage.

"We got to make something happen," I said to Goemon and also to myself.

"Hold," was all Goemon said. It was enough. The voice of reason. The steady hand. No need to gamble when you know the opponent's cards. Just let them force their own move.

He was right. My opponent peeked the window. He tried

to get crafty by leaning over to the other side. He very easily could have crawled underneath without anyone else seeing. In the end it did not matter for him. One of the dozen or so bullets I fired out of the Para lodged themselves right in the helmet, and he went down. At the same moment, I heard Goemon start firing before he even kicked the door in. He was taking no chances with reaction time firing blind like that.

The scoreboard read four left. The flank maneuver went off without a hitch. Now we had another tricky problem on our hands: assaulting a three story building with no grenades. It was possible we could peek around the corner of the barracks and land a shot through the window. If we did it that way then it all boiled down to who shot a little bit straighter and pulled the trigger a hair faster. I would be fine if it came down to that.

"We flank again," Goemon said.

"Alright. Let me peek first."

"You sure?"

"Yeah, I got this," I said. I was not feeling so confident. I felt more like all of my luck had been used up throughout the rest of the round. I was hurt bad and tired and shaky. The other duo had the upper hand. The only way to win was to be better, to be the best, and I was never the best. Why should this round be any different?

Because this was the round of destiny. It didn't matter if Goemon was the better shot. He was locked down in that barracks. If he tried to run out the door now, they would gun him down for sure. Then I would have an unwinnable 2v1 on my hands. I had to peek first, no excuses. It was the only way. Even if it meant the end for me, my partner could still win it all.

"OK," Goemon said. "Whenever you're ready."

"Now."

I was not fool enough, or hardy enough, to run out guns blazing like John Matrix. I peeked a head out around the corner at the monolith we stood to conquer. One shot, but only after I popped back behind the wall. The sound told me second floor, though that was a guess. It also told me something else.

"They're split, I think. One's on the second floor. I think. The other is looking for you."

"Let's get the clown on the second floor," Goemon said.

"But the other guy is probably waiting for you to peek."

"Doesn't matter. We can take the first down. You take the second, if he shoots me."

I hated the plan, but we had no more time. The next move of the Blue would place the Safety Circle directly on the other duo's makeshift base, handing them over the match by strategic position alone. "Fine, let's GO."

This time I channeled my inner Arnold and sprinted away from the wall. I figured they would be expecting a subdued peek again, and I wanted to throw them for a loop. I held the trigger fast, aiming from the hip to maximize my speed to try and avoid getting shot. Bullets flew everywhere. My own barrage painted the building so holy it could have been a church. My target shot up the dirt behind me. Goemon did what he needed to and lit up the guy in the window.

"He's down," Goemon said. I was elated for one quarter of one second until he continued. "Oh no. He's out the door. I'm down," he said with grave intensity. "He's coming for me but you can get him. He's going for the kill."

I shifted the gaze of the Para back towards Goemon and his aggressor. This time I used the scope. I fired at the corner of the building, preparing a stream of bullets to mow down whatever dared come outside. It was a good plan until the gun clicked.

I was out of ammo, and it would take sixteen minutes to load any more rounds into that gun. My mind flashed back to the encounter on the other side of the wall. I never reloaded the auto shotty, either. I switched over to the Revolver, the trusty Revolver, my second best friend who had been with me through it all. I lined up the iron sights and the only other survivor on the entire map spun around the corner. He was not gunning for Goemon, though, he was gunning for me.

My sights aligned on the other player's broken helmet. I pulled the trigger one time. I did not have the opportunity to pull it again, or worry about recoil or aiming the next shot. Instead, the world spiraled away from me and I left my body. Fireworks exploded into confetti-spilling shooting stars. I was still alive, but now I had a bird's eye view of the battlefield. I saw how truly small the Safety Circle had become and how close Goemon and I had come to finishing out of the top spot. I saw my own avatar, poised and ready for action that would never come, and that of the final opponent, motionless on the ground.

"What just happened," Goemon said.

"The Revolver," I said. "The Revolver happened."

The two of us screamed for a good half a minute. One hundred other people entered the arena that day. Two walked out. We won.

"I think I'm going to message that girl Elly," I said.

ABOUT THE AUTHOR

L.s. Halloway

L.S. Halloway is stranded in cyberspace. At least it gives him a chance to cover life in the digital realm from within. He holds a Theoretical Degree in Physics, but found his true passion in the school of Cyber-gonzo Journalism. His work is best consumed along a steady stream of vapor-wave. Check out book 2 in the Terra Reforma series, Side Quest Sideshow. For updates and free DLC, visit the publisher at SavageTikiTime.com.

BOOKS BY THIS AUTHOR

Terra Reforma

Terra Reforma. The post apocalyptic game world set in the period after humanity hit the reset button. A time after the bombs dropped and before society reformed into the cyberpunk megacities it consists of now. For many players, the grind of the game is more than just a brief escape from the real world. It is their perfect drug, their only way into the next rung of society or even the answer to the question of their otherwise meaningless life.

Phase Gannon, Job Class Smuggler, is too green to see the malice in NeuroCorp's game design. He just wants to hit the next quest. Kym Bit, a veteran Hacker, swears to herself and her friends IRL she will take the system down from the inside. But it will have to come after just...one... more... kill.

Phase and Kym are both looking for their own answers. Even though their paths cross in the megacity of New San Diego, the virtual wasteland of Terra Reforma holds vindication for the both of them.

A Post Apocalyptic LitRPG light and cyberpunk mashup for fans of books like New Vegas or Fallout.

Side Quest Sideshow

Phase Gannon and Kym Bit are not stuck in the game, but they might as well be. Nothing remains for either of them in the cyberpunk dystopia of real life. Besides, the post apocalyptic game world of Terra Reforma continues to boast plenty of comforts from the Old World.

Take the still-mostly-standing WonderL@nd theme park. It needs a new coat of paint or two, but the sights are worth a look so long as your armor is good enough. The park also happens to be the only thing standing between the fledgling Smuggler Phase, veteran Hacker Kym, and the land of opportunity that is Lost Angel City.

All they have to do is party up and fight their way through the four factions that reign over WonderL@nd. Maybe the team would have been better off taking the long way. Too late for that now- besides, more mobs mean more loot, right?

A Post Apocalyptic LitRPG light for fans of books like Fallout, blended with cyberpunk literature.

www.ingramcontent.com/pod-product-compliance
Lightning Source LLC
Chambersburg PA
CBHW061254120726
48001CB00001B/301